Hidden Treasures

By

ALYSIA S. KNIGHT

Hidden Treasures

By Alysia S. Knight
Published by Heart Dreams Press

Cover design: by Kelli Ann Morgan @
www.inspirecreativeservices.com

ISBN-13:978-1-942000-40-2

Also available from Alysia S. Knight

Past To Die For

Temperature Rising

Kare for Me

Blind Witness

Beauty and the Chief

Trail to Her Heart

His Governess

Her Brand of Trouble

The Ruins – Out of Time

My Spy

Whistleblower

Mindblower

Aurora Rising

Beautiful Heart

The Olympus Game

Hiding Heart

Where There's a Will

Survive the Night

To my dad who collected coins all his life
and shared his love with me.

Chapter One

"Yes!" Excitement exploded through Emily London as she spied what looked like a mixture of old jewelry, watches and keys. Embarrassed by her outburst, she glanced around to see if she'd drawn attention, or if anyone else was eyeing the ancient wooden box as she hurried toward it.

The four other people wandering the yard seemed focused on their own treasures. She was almost to her goal when a shiver ran through her. She stumbled, barely catching herself.

Emily glanced around once more, this time her gaze locked onto a man staring at her from about thirty feet away. Her breath caught as he glared. No, it had to be her imagination. He was not the type that would pay attention to a woman like her, for one thing, she was too old for him.

She doubted he was even in his mid-twenties. She was pressing thirty. His hair hung low over the collar of a very scuffed and worn leather-jacket, though it was a warm day. She, in comparison, wore white capris with a blue and white striped, V-neck, T-shirt. She looked like the girl – okay woman next door, he looked more like a thug than even a bad boy.

She shivered again. Definitely not the same type. He didn't seem the type to be at a yard sale at an old mansion either. Abruptly, he turned, shifting his gaze to a chair, proving her stereotyping wrong.

Shaking off her reaction, Emily reached her quest. Up close, the menagerie was even better than she'd hope for. The old walnut box was in even better condition than she thought. An old sewing box if she didn't miss her guess. It was a treasure in itself. She could see the possibilities, but it was the broken odds and ends that had her scooping it up.

Emily wanted to dive right in and see what goodies she could find, but there was much more the estate, correction, yard sale offered. Hoisting the box up, she settled it onto her hip so she could wander around. A lot of the other stuff was furniture. Not terribly old. There were a few knick-knacks and some books, but nothing else called to her.

Emily turned, searching for someone to pay.

Once more, she froze at the sight of another man watching her. This man was tall, six-one or two. He stood on the wide porch that wrapped around the large, southern-mansion styled house. She felt no unease. Just the opposite. Her heart lurched, drawn to him as she hadn't been to a man in months, maybe in ever.

The gentle morning breeze caught a lock of his brown hair, ruffling it up. He raised his hand to wipe the brown strands back. His eyes met hers. His lips kicked up in a bemused smile that made her breath catch.

"Can I help you?" the high cheerful voice asked.

Emily spun around to find a blonde girl about twelve years old. A hopeful smile shown on her face. Not far away stood a woman in her mid-thirties with the same intense gray eyes as her daughter. The mother was supporting the girl, but letting her take the lead.

Foolishness flashed over Emily. That was who the man had obviously been looking at, not her. He was the girl's father. Had she really been out of the dating scene so long that her heart jumped in reaction to any good looking man. He really was handsome. *Stop that. He's married, and you're not interested in relationships anymore.*

Putting on a smile of her own, Emily directed her question to the girl. “Yes, I wondered how much?”

“We were thinking fifty cents apiece, or three for a dollar,” the girl said hesitantly. Obviously afraid that would put her off.

“How much for the whole thing?”

“You want it all?” Excitement blossomed in the girl.

“I do.”

The girl looked over her shoulder to her mom.

The woman stepped forward. “What do you think, Jules?” the woman urged. “This is your project.”

“Ten dollars,” Jules said, then looked back hopeful.

“The box is worth more than that.” Emily countered back.

“That old box?” Jules studied it.

“Twenty?” Another voice chirped up. This girl was younger, about nine, with strong red hints in her hair, hazel eyes, but definitely a sister.

A little chuckle slipped from Emily. She tilted her head to the side and grinned. “How about we say forty?”

“Really?” Jules exclaimed.

“Yes. I think I saw that your poster said you were doing this as a fundraiser to help build a school.”

Both girls nodded. “Some kids can’t go to school because there isn’t one where they live. It won’t be as nice as our school. It’ll be made out of cinderblocks, but they’ll have one and we’re going to make sure it has lots of books,” Jules said, sounding very grown up.

“Well,” Emily said. “I really like to read, and I think it’s a wonderful thing you’re doing.”

The two girls beamed.

“So who do I pay?”

“Mom is handling the money,” Jules said, leading her to a table set below the steps of the big wraparound porch. “Would you like a cookie?”

“Did you make them?” Emily asked.

It was the younger sister that answered, "We both did with mom."

"I'd love a cookie. Which do you suggest, chocolate chip or sugar? I love chocolate, but a good soft sugar cookie with frosting, I think is my favorite."

"Mom's sugar cookies are the best. They're thick and soft," the little girl said authoritatively.

"It sounds like it's a sugar cookie then." Emily smiled, putting down the box to pull out her wallet.

"What are you going to do with that?" The younger girl scrunched up her nose and looked confused at the box. "All of the stuff is old and broken."

"Sara," the mom exclaimed at her daughter's bluntness.

Emily laughed. "It's all right. I get it all the time." Emily leaned down to look the girl in the eye. "I'll tell you what I do. I make jewelry and other things out of it to give it new life."

"Like what you're wearing?" Sara asked

"Yes." Emily fingered the pendant hanging on a chain around her neck. "I like to make something pretty out of old and no longer wanted stuff."

"That's beautiful." Sara reached out to touch it, then pulled her hand back, realizing she probably shouldn't.

Emily slid the chain from her neck and held it out so the girls could see.

"That's cool," Jules crowded in next to her sister.

"I'll tell you what, for an extra cookie, I'll bring you something that I make from one of the pieces in the box."

"You don't need to do that," their mother said quickly.

Emily looked at her. "I'd like to. If it's okay. I'm thinking of a hair clip."

"For me too?" Sara bounced up and down on her tiptoes.

"Sara!" her mother reprimanded, shaking her head and blushing.

Once more, Emily laughed. “One for each of you. With such beautiful hair as you have, I’ll have to make sure they’re extra special.”

“You really don’t have to do that,” their mother said again.

“They’re okay.” Emily winked. “Besides, you let me throw in the box which is a great piece. I think I’m getting a much better end of this deal. “I’m Emily London.” She held out her hand.

“Payton North. Mother of these two.” There was pleasure as she glanced at her daughters.

“This is a great place.” Emily looked at the magnificent, old house.

“It was my grandfather’s. It’s my brother’s now. Somehow these two came up with the idea to earn money when they were helping him clean out the attic.”

“Well. This is incredible,” Emily said.

“I’m afraid it’s just the start.” A warm baritone voice said over her shoulder.

“Uncle Quinn, Uncle Quinn, we got forty dollars for the box,” Sara said with youthful exuberance.

“That’s wonderful.” He turned his attention to the girl, whose head was bobbing up and down.

“She’s going to make things with the junk. She’s going to make me a barrette, like she made her necklace. Isn’t it pretty?”

He turned his attention to Emily. “It is very beautiful.”

Emily felt her heart jump as if the compliment was directed at her, not the necklace. His eyes were hazel, the most intriguing eyes she’d ever seen. The outside were a mixture of blues and greens, the center almost an amber color. *Get a hold of yourself. Uncle, not father. Was he married? It doesn’t matter. I’ve sworn off men.* Still, she couldn’t stop herself from noticing he didn’t wear a wedding ring.

"So, Emily," Payton broke in. "What do you do for work when you're not remaking things."

"That's actually what I do. I have several shops that carry my creations, plus an online business." Emily shifted her attention back to the woman. "It's called Beautiful Again."

"As Sara said, 'cool'. Where'd you come up with the idea?" Payton asked.

"My grandmother. She was always doing crafts with things she had around."

"Your husband must like that, having a hobby you get paid for," Payton said.

"I'm not married. Oh –." Emily cutoff, her attention going beyond her to a man reaching toward the box she'd purchased. She took the couple steps to the table. "I'm sorry, but I already bought that." When he turned, Emily found herself looking at the man that gave her the creeps earlier.

The muscles around his dark-brown eyes tightened. "The whole box?" There was a snide snap to his voice.

Emily stiffened. "Yes." She reached for it, lifting it once more to rest on her hip.

"Sorry," the man rumbled.

Emily didn't get the feeling he was at all sorry. In fact, she was certain he knew she had purchased it.

"I collect old keys. I saw several in there. I'll give you five bucks for any skeleton type keys." He didn't seem to blink as he stared.

A chill ran through her. "No, thanks."

"Hey, I'll make it apiece. It's a good deal. Probably as much as you paid for the junk," he countered.

"No, thanks," Emily said again, tightening her hold on the sewing box.

His jaw clenched, then he glanced over her shoulder. "I guess there is nothing that interests me here then." He turned and strode across the wide expanse of lawn to the road.

"Well, that was rude," Payton said, "I mean not as much of what he said, just how."

"Yes," Quinn agreed.

Emily hadn't realized he'd moved up beside her, but felt a warm comfort from his presence. She tried to shrug her unease away, but had to fight to keep from looking after the man. "Collectors can be somewhat obsessive if they see something they want. Unfortunately for him, I really like to use old keys. I think I'll take this down and put it in my car." She bumped it up a bit more on her hip.

"What about your cookies?" Sara, still standing by her mom, asked.

She's so adorable. The tension eased from Emily's muscles. "I'll be right back. I want to look around a bit more."

"If you have time, why don't you join us on the veranda for some lemonade?" Payton invited.

"Yes." Sara practically squeaked.

Emily smiled down at the girl who was bouncing up and down again with excitement. "How can I refuse? Thank you. I'll be right back."

Emily walked down the curved driveway, through the stone pillars that stood on either side. Her car was only about twenty-five feet from the entrance, but with the trees and shrubs she couldn't see the house tucked away.

What an amazing place. She guessed it would be considered one step down from a mansion. It wasn't overly grandiose, just large and well-designed, so that though old, it held a timeless appeal. She'd love to investigate it.

Unlocking her small SUV, Emily placed the box in the back. Temptation hit her again to explore the contents. Unable to stop herself, she picked up a couple pieces. Ideas swam in her mind, then she saw the small, enameled dragonfly pin.

"Oh," she gasped, reaching up to finger the dragonfly on the necklace she wore. It had become her symbol the day she started to remake herself, from the moment when she walked away from her previous life, her career, and her fiancé.

"Everything can be remade." Her grandmother had told her often enough when they'd sit and do crafts together. *"You'll find, even we have to change, evolve, grow. The challenge is transforming ourselves into what we really want to be. What we're meant to be. That truly is the challenge of life."* Her grandmother's words came clearly to her mind, followed by the image of the man – Uncle Quinn.

Chapter Two

Thank you, Sis. Quinn Lawson watched the woman walk down the drive. Payton might be a little sneaky and was probably matchmaking, but he couldn't say he regretted it. *She wasn't married.*

Emily London was beautiful, but not in the flashy way, but the natural way. Her hair was not truly blonde or brown but a mixture of the two. At the moment it was pulled back into a ponytail, but freed, he guessed her hair would hang several inches down her back. Her eyes a clear blue, darker rimmed and paler in the center. He couldn't help miss how striking they were.

Her looks had caught him the moment he'd first seen her, drawing him around the porch, spellbound. He hadn't had a woman catch his attention like that in a long time, but what held it was the way she'd talked to his nieces.

She smiled and even laughed openly with them. Lowering to look at them straight on, instead of dismissing them.

"Uncle Quinn," Sara drew his attention. "We're doing good."

"Is that right?" He swung her up.

"Ah huh. We sold the dresser, desk and bed to one person."

"That's great."

"Mom, someone is interested in the chairs and couch," Jules called to their mother, and Sara squirmed to get down to run join them.

Quinn smiled after her. She was a bundle of energy, who always had to be in the middle of everything. His gazed shifted, honing in on Emily as she came around the stone pillar. She had a quick fluid stride that didn't waste time covering the ground.

Sara saw her and shifted directions to intercept, catching her hand, pulling her forward. Evidently he wasn't the only one drawn to the woman. Inside he cautioned himself, but still stepped to greet her as Sara led her up the steps.

"Mind if I join you two?"

Surprise flickered over Emily's face and he thought he detected a slight blush when she nodded.

"You sit here, and I'll get you some punch and cookies," Sara said, hurrying back down the stairs.

Quinn liked the little laugh that escaped the woman. "Is she always like that?"

"A little whirlwind? Yes. She's been keeping her parents hopping from the day she was born." He held the chair of a bistro table that the girls had moved from the side garden. "Jules was a much more docile child. Even as a baby. She loves to read and play the piano. I have a feeling if Sara goes for an instrument it will be the drums. Right now, she's into gymnastics. By the way, I'm Quinn Lawson." He held out his hand.

"Emily London."

She reached over the table, placing her hand in his. His whole world shifted. He wondered if hers did too as he heard a small gasp slip from her lips. All he knew was that he didn't want to release her.

Sara came up, walking carefully not to drop the plate of cookies she had balancing on one of the glasses.

Emily released his hand, color flaring on her cheeks as she reached for the plate. “Thank you,” Emily said, putting it in the center of the table before taking the offered glass. “The cookies look wonderful.”

“They are. Mommy makes the best.”

“With your help?”

“I put the sprinkles on. Jules did the frosting. I need to go help her now if someone has a question.” The girl bounded down the stairs.

Quinn watched her go, wondering if someone else was matchmaking. He loved his nieces. “So you like old keys?”

“Actually, I really do.” Emily picked up a cookie. “They make such interesting additions to what I make.”

“I didn’t realize that box was in there. As you can see most was furniture.”

“Oh, if you didn’t plan to sell it –”

“No.” He cut her off. “It’s okay. One of the girls must have put it there.”

“Well, if I find anything really valuable, I’ll return it.”

Quinn was shocked at the offer and that he believed her. “That’s not necessary,” he said but knew she still would. He studied her.

She looked over the yard. “It looks like their sale is going well.”

He followed her gaze. “It is.” Over half the stuff was gone or had sold signs.

“So all this came from the house?”

“Yes. They were helping me clean some things out. I was going to haul some away and Jules came up with the idea. I thought why not. I was going to donate it to charity anyway, so if they earn some money that’s fine.”

“That’s nice of you.”

He shrugged. “I was just cleaning it out. My grandfather used to store old furniture in the attic when he got something new, just in case it was needed again.”

“You inherited this from your grandfather?”

He played with his glass, running his finger around the rim. "He passed away a year ago. He was eighty-six."

"You were close." It wasn't a question.

"Yeah, I used to spend summers here. Loved it. He got lung cancer, though he never smoked a day in his life. He was always a healthy, robust man, until the last year. We moved him down to Arizona to my parent's house when he got sick."

"So you grew up in Arizona?"

He laughed. "I'm making this confusing, aren't I?" He took a drink. "In my early years we only lived about twenty miles from here, but my father was in construction, so if he was on a project somewhere, we would usually go there. My parents like to be together."

"That must have been rough. Changing schools all the time."

He shrugged. "Not bad. For elementary, we were home schooled. My mom was a teacher before she met my dad. She made sure we got a real good base, and we were always in sports to give us plenty of exercise and friends. For my junior high years, which coincided with Payton's high school, we stayed in one place. Then another for my high school. So that's my story, how about yours?"

"Mine's a little more boring, I grew up in the same house, went to the same school all along. I played a lot of sports to keep busy."

"Really, what sports?"

"Volleyball, soccer, tennis, a little basketball, but I wasn't very good at that. Too hyper."

"So that's why Sara's attached to you, kindred spirits."

She laughed. "Maybe. She's so cute."

"You have any nieces and nephews?"

"Yes, but we're not close. I was a later in life surprise for my parents. They're both gone now. I have two older brothers, one was married and had moved away before I came along. I have a nephew a year older and a niece a year younger there, and my other brother was just heading to college. So I have two more nephews and a niece from him, but he went into international business and lived in Japan, and we never got to be close either."

"You grew up mostly an only child."

"Yep." Emily said easily.

Quinn wasn't sure when their eyes locked, but he didn't want to take his gaze off her. There was such a sweetness to her. Natural, the thought came to him again. Just how it felt being with her.

She broke contact looking away. A blush stole over her cheeks. "I guess I should be going." She glanced up and smiled again. "Thanks for the visit."

Quinn didn't want her to leave, especially without her number. He rose as she did. "I'm just starting to go through things. This was just getting rid of some so I have room to work. There might be more jewelry and keys." He grinned. "If you'd be interested, I could give you a call."

"That would be wonderful. If you don't mind?"

"Not at all. If you'll give me your number." He pulled out his phone. Emily rattled it off as he put it in, then before he gave himself time to think, he opened the camera. "Smile."

He caught the picture before she could think about being self-conscious about it. "You don't mind, do you? I can erase it if you do."

She blushed and shook her head. "No, it's okay." She sounded a little breathless.

"You know it's fair play if you want to take mine." He couldn't believe he said it.

"True." She cocked her head to the side, her lips curving up. She pulled out her phone and before he had a chance to pose snapped a picture.

"Come on. You at least need to give me a chance to smile."

"Okay, smile." She took another shot. "I better go now so you can get back to what you were doing." There was a touch of hesitancy in her voice.

"Thanks for letting me join you. I hope to find something so I have an excuse to call you." *I'll find something, if I have to tear the whole house apart.*

"Bye." The word sounded a little breathless.

It pulled at him.

She went down the steps, glancing back over her shoulder as she reached the bottom and smiled. She stopped on her way across the yard to talk with Payton and both girls, receiving a hug from Sara.

ଓ෴ဢ

Emily fingered her phone, tempted to look at the pictures she'd just took of Quinn Lawson. Instead she continued her way down the drive after saying goodbye to the girls and their mother.

It was such an amazing day. She hadn't planned on going to any yard sales. Hadn't even known about this one. But she'd taken a wrong turn after making a delivery, seen the sign, and had been prompted to stop. Now, she had a chest in her car full of intriguing possibilities and met an even more intriguing man. She could be honest about that. Plus, she made what she felt, were a couple friends.

She turned onto the road. Feeling a bit fanciful, she wondered if fate had brought her there. No! What was she thinking? She was off men. She stopped, buried her face in her hands. "Oh." She let out a breath, gliding her hands back over her hair while trying to steady her foolish heart.

Starting forward again, she rounded some bushes and caught sight of her car with a man standing beside it. There was a thump accompanied by breaking glass.

"Hey!" Emily yelled, starting forward, then pulled back as the foolishness of the move hit her, but it was too late. The man dove for her, catching her arm and spinning her back. Emily screamed at the sight of the crowbar coming toward her.

She swung up her arms. The crowbar hit her purse instead of her head. When he pulled back to swing again, it hooked her purse strap. He lost his grip of the crowbar as he yanked her purse from her grip. Both items went flying, and he struck with his hand instead.

The blow clipped her chin bringing tears to her eyes. Emily kicked, then hit, trying to break free.

He grunted, jerked her around, blocking her fist as she tried to hit again. His strike was more effective.

Emily glimpsed cruel features before his hand caught the side of her head, knocking her to the ground. The world blurred and faded away.

Chapter Three

A distant yell broke the air just as Quinn turned toward the house. *Emily.* Her name burst through his mind. He leapt off the steps and ran across the yard instead of going down the drive. Quinn cut through the bushes, dodging trees.

A cry sounded just ahead only to be cut-off abruptly.

Quinn reached the low stone fence that bordered the property and vaulted over it, landing on the road in time to see a man in jeans and a leather jacket struggling with Emily.

"Freeze!" Quinn shouted running toward them. To his surprise, the man froze for a split second, then before Quinn could reach them the man struck Emily on the side of her head and released her.

Emily fell to the ground, going still.

The man bolted to a motorcycle and kicked it to life. The motorcycle roared down the street. The frustration of not catching the man flew from Quinn's mind at the sight of Emily on the ground by her car.

He ran to her and dropped down. "Emily."

There was no movement. He reached for his cellphone in his pocket, and realized he'd left it on the table. He brushed her cheek, wiping back a few tendrils of hair that had come loose from their restraint, conscious of the reddening mark. "Emily," he said her name again gently.

She shifted slightly and a small whimper escaped.

"That's it Emily. Come on. Open your eyes. You can do it. Look at me." To his relief, she did. Her eyelashes fluttered a couple times then stay opened. Her little gasp and flash of panic eased as her eyes locked on him.

"It's okay."

"Quinn?" Confusion replaced the look of fear.

He'd never been so happy to hear his name. "It's all right. Lay still."

"What?" She started to raise her hand to touch her head, but he caught it, holding it against his chest.

"It's all right. I dare say you're going to have a bruise on your jaw. Just be still a moment so I know you're all right, then I'll carry you back to the house and call the police."

"The police? The man. My car!" She jerked, trying to shift.

"No, stay still." He held her down. "It's okay."

She let out a little groan and closed her eyes a moment, then with a deep breath opened them. "I'm okay now. Really," she added, obviously reading his thoughts.

When she tried to rise again, he helped her. "Just to sitting."

She made it, but he slid his arm behind her to steady her.

"My car."

He looked over. The shattered window told the whole story. She came upon someone trying to break in. He needed to call the police, though he wasn't sure what good it would do. The man was long gone, though besides theft, assault might up the hunt for him.

"I left my cellphone in the house. Do you have one?"

She went to nodded then stopped with a gasp. "My pocket."

He took the cellphone when she pulled it out and called 911. Emily rejected the need for an ambulance, but

Quinn was assured by the dispatcher that a paramedic would be there with the police to check her out.

"Just stay still until they get here," he said when Emily went to get up again, then moved behind her so she could relax against his leg. Now that his initial reaction was fading, his awareness to her heightened once more. The urge to lift her into his arms and cuddle her was strong. All he wanted was to carry her up to his house where he could lock out the world and keep her safe.

He didn't know where the instinct was coming from. He'd never been the over-protective, caveman type, not even with his ex-fiancée, who loved playing the helpless, china doll. If anything, it had irritated him. Emily wasn't at all like that, but he wanted to guard her.

Fortunately, before he could do something stupid, a police car came around the bend, pulling to a stop in front of Emily's car.

"Mr. Lawson?" the officer asked getting out of his car.

"Yes, and this is Emily London."

"You okay, Miss?" He directed his attention to her.

Emily nodded. "Yes." This time when she tried to rise, Quinn helped her. Slightly unsteady, she gripped his arm.

Quinn was only too happy to hold her.

"I'm Officer Carlson. Are you sure you're all right? We have a unit on the way to check you out." The officer was only a little taller than Emily, solidly built, with close-cropped, dark hair. He carried his authority well, confident but not arrogant. There was true concern in him.

"I'm fine. Just a little shaky," Emily said.

"He hit her. I saw it before I could stop him." Quinn added.

"Why don't you come sit down over here in my cruiser and you can tell me what happened?" He motioned, but just then the paramedic vehicle came around the curve. "Change of plan. How about we let them check you out and I'll talk to Mr. Lawson first?"

Her protest was cut off as they walked her to the ambulance as the two paramedics climbed out to meet them.

"Let's just let them check you out," the police officer encouraged.

Emily was settled on the back of the vehicle while the men did a quick examination.

"Can you tell me what you saw?" Officer Carlson urged Quinn away from the rescue vehicle so the men could work.

Quinn went over everything.

"So it was the shout that drew you?" The officer stopped him. "What did she say?"

"Honestly, I don't know." Quinn shrugged. "I don't know why it alerted me. It just did."

"Did you recognize the man?"

"No, I'd say average height, maybe five-ten. Slightly stocky. Shaggy hair. Jeans. Leather jacket. That's all I got, but I think he was at the yard sale earlier."

"Yard sale?" Officer Carlson cocked an eyebrow.

"My nieces are having it." Quinn motioned toward the house. "Miss London was there. She bought a box full of pieces of old jewelry."

"Valuable?"

"No, just odds and ends."

"Did the man take it?

Quinn thought for a second. "I don't think so. He didn't have anything in his hand when he hit her, and I didn't see anything when he got on the motorcycle. I wish I could give you a better description, I only caught a glimpse. All I can say was it was a black motorcycle. Not sure of the make. It wasn't a Harley or a bullet type. The first and the last numbers on the plate were zeros.

"Was it all numbers or were there letters?" the officer asked with interest.

"There were letters, I just couldn't catch them."

"Then, it's likely the last was the letter O, not a zero. It's how our plates are commonly set up. Unless it was personalized."

"I don't think so. I would have registered that. I tried when I realized I wasn't going to catch him."

"You did well. Most people can't give that much. Though the main thing here is Miss London is all right."

Together they moved over to the ambulance.

"How's she doing, Mike?" Carlson asked.

"She's elected not to go to the hospital, and we're not seeing anything to force the issue, though I'd suggest she take it easy for a day or two. No heavy lifting or climbing." The paramedic looked to Emily stressing the words.

"Can I speak to her then?" Carlson motioned to Emily.

"She's all yours." The EMT nodded.

Carlson first let her tell what happened, then as he did with Quinn, he asked questions, pulling out more information.

"So when you first saw the man he hadn't got in your car?"

"No, he'd just broke out the window and started to reach in to unlock it I guess," Emily said.

"You said he used a crowbar, but he didn't hit you with it?" Officer Carlson asked.

Emily was quiet a moment as she went over everything in her mind. Her breathing became more rapid. "He was going to, but I threw up my hands and he hit my purse instead." She looked around, obviously thinking of it for the first time.

Quinn turned and scanned the area. He saw the large, blue and white canvas bag she'd been carrying earlier about ten feet from her car in the shrubs. "There it is."

Emily visibly relaxed at the sight of it. When she started to move, Quinn raised his hand to stop her. "I'll get it." He walked over and picked it up. As he did there was a clatter.

"Wait!" Carlson stopped him, coming over. Pulling on gloves, he lifted the strap, untangling the crowbar.

Quinn stared at the object going cold inside. If Emily would have been hit with that, well, he didn't want to think of the outcome. The grimness of the officer stressed the thought.

After Officer Carlson placed the crowbar in an evidence bag and put it in his car, he came back to her. "Can you describe what he was wearing?"

Her description matched, but she hadn't seen the motorcycle.

"Mr. Lawson said he thought he was at the yard sale," the officer probed.

"Yes, I'll never forget his eyes." She shivered. "It was disturbing when I saw him watching me."

"He was watching you?"

"Yes, at least I thought he was." She looked uncertain.

"When was this?" Carlson studied her.

"Right after I first got there. I was just walking around and saw a box of what looked like bits and pieces of jewelry. I looked around to see if anyone else was heading toward it. That's when I saw him. After I'd purchased the box, he tried to get into it, but I thought he'd left."

Quinn watched as Carlson made a few notes then looked to him. "Did you notice him then?"

"I didn't pay him any attention," Quinn said. *I was busy watching her.* "My sister might have, but I don't know if she can give you anything else useful."

"Let me take a few pictures here then I'd like to talk to your sister to see if she can add anything," Officer Carlson said before stepping away to do so.

Quinn's attention went to Emily, not that it had been far from her. She swayed a little, placing her hand on the vehicle for balance.

"Hey." Quinn reached for her, sliding his arm around her to steady her. "Why don't I carry you up to the house?"

"No, I'm fine, just a touch woozy. I don't want to leave my car here. Especially with the broken window."

"When he's done, I'll drive it up to the house and see if I can get someone out to fix it." Quinn couldn't help but notice how good she felt by his side or the way she placed her hand against his chest for balance.

"You don't need to go to that trouble," she protested.

"I feel a little responsible. You were at my house when this happened."

"I'd left your house," she pointed out.

"Moot point. Besides, if it were my sister, I would hope someone would help her."

Emily sighed, not able to argue with that. "Thank you for being so kind and coming to my rescue."

"You're welcome," he said just as the officer walked toward them.

"I'm going to talk to your sister."

"Is it all right if I move the car?" Quinn asked.

"Sure. I'm done here."

"I'm going to take Miss London up to the house to rest a while and make sure she's steady before she leaves."

"That's a good idea. I was going to ask if she had someone who could come get her, or be with her a while."

"We'll watch over her," Quinn added quickly before she could protest. Taking her arm, he guided her to the driver's side and opened the door to the back seat. "I figured this would be better than sitting in the glass. Keys?" He held out his hand.

She surprised him when she didn't argue at all but just handed them over.

☙❧

Once more, Emily sat on the porch of the stately house, but instead of at the bistro table, she reclined on a padded lounger, only half listening to the conversation going on below her.

"I didn't hear anything." Payton was telling the officer. "Quinn all of a sudden jumped off the porch and took off through the trees. I thought he came to his senses and ran after her to ask her out."

The likelihood of thought hit Emily. *Quinn Lawson, asking her out. Right. The man was gorgeous and nice.* He'd been so caring when he'd settled her there. Getting her a glass of water, ice pack and something for her headache. She hated the fact that he felt responsible for what happened.

"... for the man. I remember him," Payton added giving her description.

A shudder went through her. Emily wished she could forget him.

The conversation continued. "I thought he left," Payton continued. "But while I was helping someone else, I caught sight of him walking around, looking at everything, I mean everyone was looking, but it seemed more like he was hunting for something. I do remember that several times he looked toward Emily on the porch. I wondered if he was trying to get up enough courage to approach her again. His earlier attempt was awkward. In fact, plain rude."

"Did you talk to him?" Carlson asked.

"No, he didn't seem interested in anything except the box Emily bought. He disappeared not long before she left."

Emily closed her eyes and drifted. She didn't know how much time had passed. The images of Quinn Lawson filled her mind. The way he smiled that made an intriguing dimple form just on his right cheek. His amazing eyes were the most striking combination of blues, greens and golds. She came awake staring into those eyes. Emily sighed, wanting to get lost in them forever.

"Sorry. The man is finished with your car window and needs your signature." Quinn crouched next to her.

"Oh." The shock of the reality of his words hit her. "Sorry. I didn't mean to fall asleep." She sat up, then worked her jaw, grimacing.

"It's an interesting shade of blue and purple you got there, but not as bad as I feared." He started to raise his hand to touch her cheek, then paused, his finger an inch away.

She felt herself blush at the intensity in his eyes. "The ice helped."

He stood and held out his hand to assist her up. They were strong hands, not overly rough, but showed he wasn't afraid of hard work. When she swayed toward him as she rose, it wasn't from dizziness but the pull on her heart.

What was happening to her? The hint of musk and sandalwood reached her along with a pleasant masculine scent she figured was all his own. Never had she felt a draw like this.

Not even Greg, her ex-fiancé, who was supposed to be right for her, the man she was going to spend the rest of her life with. Greg's hands had been soft, too soft. It had annoyed her. *Stop!* She needed to get herself back under control.

"Thank you." She straightened, jerking back her hand.

He stepped back, tipping his head to the side, in an action that almost shouted confusion.

"I really better go." She wrapped her arms around herself to keep from reaching for him. "You've been more than kind, but I've taken up too much of your time." She fought the urge to lean into him. She really had to get out of there. The day had her totally off-balance. "I … thank you." She fled down the steps and out to meet the repair man who was standing by her car.

Emily quickly signed the papers. She turned to wave good-bye to Payton and the girls. Unable to stop herself, her gaze went to the man still standing on the porch, his hands buried in his pocket. She wanted to go back to him. Instead, she climbed in her car and drove off.

Chapter Four

"What did you do?" Payton's voice jerked Quinn from his reverie.

Quinn blew out a breath. "I don't know. She just … left."

"More like fled. You've lost your touch brother," she teased. "At least, tell me you got her phone number this time?"

"I got it before," he said, feeling a touch testy. Had he done something? He'd been out of the dating market for a while, but he didn't think he was that rusty. They'd seemed to be getting along fine. He blew out another breath. And, then she was attacked. Of all the luck. He found what he thought was a nice, interesting, beautiful woman and their meeting was marred.

"Hey," Payton drew his attention. "It's okay. I was just teasing you."

Quinn realized he must've missed something. "Yeah."

"I liked her."

"I did, too." It was more than that, his insides fairly shouted.

"Then, give it time. Call her in a day or two, just to check up on how she's doing," she suggested.

"The thought already crossed my mind." Though he really didn't want to wait that long.

"See there's still hope for you." Payton patted his cheek. "Oh, do you want to come give us a hand loading?" She motioned to a truck that just pulled up the driveway.

"Sure." He stared down the road where Emily disappeared a moment longer before following his sister.

ᴏᴓᴔᴏ

Emily stood on the porch of the estate once again, her finger over the doorbell, debating if she dared ring it after the way she'd fled the day before. Her mind had been in a complete whirl since she'd left, and at the center of the spiral was Quinn Lawson.

Driving away, she had convinced herself he would fade from her mind, but it hadn't been so. He had taken up residence in her thoughts. She couldn't even escape him in her dreams or awake and working. Usually when creating, she became so focused the world slipped away, but not Quinn Lawson.

Maybe Payton would answer the door and she wouldn't have to see him. Did she want to see him? She didn't know. Maybe if she did, he wouldn't be as interesting as her mind made him seem – or maybe he would, then what was she going to do? She was off men. She couldn't trust them, especially the good looking ones that made her heart pound.

You can't just stand here. Someone's probably watching you on the security camera. She glanced at it. *Ring the bell. Maybe no one's home and you can leave the barrettes with a note.*

Not giving herself any more time, she leaned into the button. A delightful, musical chime sounded from inside.

Emily was just wondering if she could chicken out, when the door opened.

"Emily." Her name sounded like pleasure in Quinn's greeting.

Whatever attempt she'd made in her mind to convince herself that he wasn't as attractive as she remembered, was wrong. True, he wasn't drop-dead gorgeous, but he was good looking, in kind of a rugged way. At least, she considered him so. He wore jeans and a T-shirt, and there was a smudge of dirt on his cheek.

"Sorry, I didn't mean to disturb you."

"You're not. Come on in." He opened the door wide, letting her see in to the opulent entry. Rich wood and a glistening chandelier beckoned her.

"I don't want to intrude. I just have something for Jules and Sara."

"They're not here. They live about twenty minutes from here."

"Oh, well, you can just give it to them, when you see them." She held out two small paper gift bags, one pink, one lavender, with raffia streaming from the handles.

"Tell you what," Quinn said, not reaching for the bags. "If you're not too busy, how about taking a ride with me, and we can deliver them."

Emily wanted to say yes. "I don't want to interrupt you."

"Believe me, you're not. I could use a break. I'm just going through stuff. Most of it is junk, but there are a few things I want to keep, so it's a long process. Please, Emily," he said when she hesitated.

"If I'm really not bothering you, I'd love to."

"Great." He looked down at his hands. "I better wash up first." He opened the door wider, motioning her inside.

The gleaming hardwood floor carried into a formal living room, with a large marble fireplace flanked by large windows that filled the room with light.

"This is beautiful." Emily turned, taking it in. "Just the right touch of old and new."

"My mother would be pleased with the compliment. She did it a couple years ago when we renovated the house."

"She did an amazing job."

"My parents used to split their time between living here and Arizona. She insisted it be modernized, but keep its charm."

"She accomplished her goal." Emily ran her finger over an inlaid table.

"Feel free to look around. I'll hurry and wash up and we can leave." He stopped in the doorway before heading down the hallway and turned back. "Do you have to be back at any certain time?"

"No, I'm done for the day."

"Good. Would you like to have dinner with me? There's a steakhouse we can stop at on our way back," he added on. "Or if you're in the mood for something else, I'm up for suggestions."

"You can't ever go wrong with steak." She smiled, flutters bursting inside her.

"My thoughts exactly. Be right back."

Emily couldn't take her eyes off the hall, the alluring treasures in the room forgotten at the thought of going to dinner with Quinn.

True to his word, he was back a few minutes later, minus the smudge on his face. "Ready?"

"Yes."

"My car's out this way." He pointed down the hallway.

She followed him, having to fight not to stop and investigate, especially when they passed a large, modern-country styled kitchen that opened to a family-room with floor to ceiling windows. That was the type of room she wanted when she started house hunting. He held a door open for her, and she hurried forward.

Emily stepped out into a breezeway to the garage. Glass panels were pushed back leaving it open air at the moment, but in winter could be closed up. On one side it let out onto the wrap around porch to the front of the house, the other side was a flower lined path to the back.

She stopped and just looked around, trying to take it in. “What a great idea. I would’ve never guessed from the front of the house.” She figured she’d had to rethink her first thought of not quite a mansion.

“I think I told you my great-grandfather built it for my great-grandmother.”

“This is genius and so charming.” She stopped at a rose bush and leaned in to smell a flower. “Your grandmother must have loved it.”

“From what I was told, she did. They lived here only fourteen years then she died in child birth.”

“That’s sad.”

“Yeah, even when you think it happened often back then, it had to be hard. She was great-grandfather’s love. He always said she was his greatest treasure. Out back in the woods there is a memorial he built for her. He used to go sit out there all the time. I’ll show you later if you’d like, but for now my nieces, then dinner.”

He led her into a garage that could have held six vehicles but there were only two parked there. A red truck that was only two or three-years-old, next to a shiny new blue luxury performance sedan. He opened the door to the sedan, and handed her in, then went around to the driver’s side.

“Nice car,” she said as he got in.

“Thanks, I got her when I moved here.”

“Her? Does she have a name?”

“Hmmm, maybe I’ll tell you sometime.” He shot her a grin. “Where’s your car?”

“I only live a couple streets from here. Maybe a mile, so decided to walk.”

“Really?” He arched an eyebrow.

“I needed to get a little exercise after working all morning, and I like to walk. Also, that way I can get a feel of the neighborhood. I’m renting a place until I decide if I like the area.”

"So how long have you lived here?"

"About four months. I needed a change, to get out of the city, start over, and remake myself."

"Something happened?"

"A lot." She paused a moment. "I went to school for business. I was going to take the world by storm, and I was pretty much on track to where I wanted to be." She broke off, feeling the weight of it descend on her.

"Do you mind if I ask what happened? It's all right if you don't want to talk about it." He glanced her way then back to the road.

Emily was silent a second more, letting it play through her mind. Funny, for the first time, it didn't hurt like it usually did. "I did an internship with a company, did well and they hired me. I moved up rapidly. Helped land a couple big accounts. As to the life script, I got engaged. He worked at the company, a co-worker. Not my boss, but a level up, going for vice-president. I know not smart."

"But you were in love." He gave her the way out, but she couldn't take it.

"I … I don't think I ever was. Everyone said we were perfect. I thought it was meant to be. It fit my perfect plan."

"So what happened?"

"Higher ups made some bad decisions so they had to cut back. I was one of the ones who got cut. I knew I'd be okay. I had a solid resume, but was upset and went to see my fiancé." She grimaced but continued. "Let's just say I picked an inopportune moment." She wrinkled her nose. "He was with my secretary, not even his."

"I would say it was the opportune time," Quinn said emphatically.

"Yes. He actually had the audacity to blame it on me." Her ire rising. "Because I wanted to wait for our wedding night. He said just because I wouldn't sleep with him, didn't mean he should go without."

"I'll be nice and just say, jerk."

She smiled, her tension fading. "Yes. The thing is, I promised my Grandmother I'd wait. Silly, old fashioned, I know, but I did and wanted to keep my word. My grandmother was one of the wisest women I've ever known. Looking back though, I can also admit, I didn't want to sleep with him. I didn't feel right about it. I think, subconsciously, I knew the whole thing was wrong. Anyway." She shrugged. "It was a rude awakening. I realized I wasn't being true to myself. I'd lost myself in the push to succeed or what I thought of as success."

"So you remade yourself."

Emily could swear she heard admiration in his voice. "I'm trying to. I sold my condo. Pretty much threw a dart at the map and ended up here. I like it. I have a couple months more on my lease and am starting to look for a place to buy."

"Another condo or townhouse?" He pulled over and parked.

"No. Something more me. I want a house. I want a yard. I'd like a place I could make a workshop that's not my garage or extra bedroom. That's why I picked this area. Not as modern. A little more land, a little more country or with a more old-fashion feel."

"You'll probably end up needing to update some."

"That's fine. I'm pretty good at that. I got my condo for a steal and did most the work on it myself."

"Handy with tools, hah?"

"Yep. My father was a true jack-of-all-trades. People in my old life would have been shocked."

"They didn't know?"

"No. That type of thing wouldn't have been acceptable. As I said, I couldn't be myself. So now I am, and I'm content. Happier than I was ever then. I can't believe I just told you all that." She blushed.

"I'm glad you did."

You idiot. She chided herself. What a dope she was, going on like that.

ꟹ

Quinn wanted to turn and just stare at Emily. He wondered if she realized how much she'd just revealed about herself. She was amazing. He wanted to hear more, unfortunately they'd just reached his sister's street.

"We're here." He pulled over in front of a large, new-traditional style house, dismissing the urge to detour around the neighborhood just to spend more time talking.

"This is nice."

"It is. It's a newer subdivision of up-scale houses. Payton's was one of the first built. It's a nice area, but probably not what you're looking for."

"You're right, but they are beautiful homes. Not cookie-cutter."

"Payton's husband, Richard, is an architect. A good one. He designs all the homes here. He customizes each to the owner's specifications."

"Wow. Kind of the old fashioned way."

"Exactly," Quinn said with pride. Getting out to come around the car for her. His family's company built good homes, even in the lower priced homes they kept the same quality. It was a family tradition, started by his great-grandfather, all the way back before the depression.

"So, which do you prefer?" she asked as she stood. "You said you inherited your grandfather's house. Are you going to keep it?

"Yes." There was no thought in that. "That's one of the reasons it was given to me. Richard built my sister her dream house. But for me, I've always had a pull to the old house. The history has always felt part of me. I know it's really not much of a bachelor's place."

"I don't see anything wrong with it."

"I know it's not for everyone, many want the new gleaming look. Payton's a little that way."

"Well, the nice thing is, it's okay whichever you like."

"I'll give you a complete tour sometime," Quinn said, thinking of maneuvering it into a second date.

"I'd love it," Emily said just before the door opened.

"Uncle Quinn." Sara launched herself into his arms, which he luckily got out in time to catch her.

"Quinn." Payton came hurrying down the hall after her daughter.

"I didn't know you were coming by," Payton said, wiping her hand on a towel. "I was just making dinner. Want to stay?"

"Can't. I have other plans. I just came bearing gifts, or at least, I brought someone bearing gifts." He settled Sara on his hip and moved to reveal Emily.

"Emily." Sara shifted so she could see her, then reached for her.

It was a good thing Emily had good reflexes, because if she expected just a hug, she got a whole eight-year-old instead.

"You brought me something." The squeal was back, as Sara twisted trying to see the bags that were now behind her.

"Sara." Payton groaned.

Emily smiled, unable to resist the infectious child. "I think we should wait for Jules?"

"Jules!" Sara turned and yelled for her sister.

Payton sighed and shook her head. "Would you like to come in?" She then looked at her daughter. "Why don't you run and find your sister instead of just yelling?"

Emily put her down, and Sara took off into the back of the house. "Your house is lovely." Emily looked around admiringly as they went under an archway back into a family room. Windows spanned the wall and stretched from the floor to the top of the two-story high ceiling, which seemed to bring the outdoors in. "Quinn said your husband designed this."

"He did and got it just perfect." Payton smiled with pride.

The girls came running into the room.

"Hi," Jules greeted.

"Hi. I wanted to deliver something to you, and your uncle volunteered to drive me out." Emily handed the lavender bag to Jules and the pink to Sara.

"Oh, wow, it's a dragonfly." Jules fingered the barrette Emily created.

"Look at mine," Sara exclaimed. "Mine's a mouse."

"Those are beautiful." Payton looked over her daughter's shoulder. "Those are really neat. I can't believe you made them out of that junk."

"Those are cool," Quinn leaned in to study them.

Emily laughed. "That's what I do."

"You also made your necklace," Jules said with certainty.

Attention turned to the necklace she wore as Emily reached to finger it. An old key hung with a collection of pearls, crystals and charms, and an ever present dragonfly when she made something for herself. "I did."

"So that's what you meant, by liking to use skeleton keys," Quinn said.

"Yes, they're so simple but interesting. I don't know how to explain it. I don't get authentic ones often. I can buy a lot of reproductions and use them for accents, but I love it when I can get a key like this one. It was in your box. It's beautiful. So original. The two hearts intertwine. Look at the workmanship in it, and it's just a key. I decided to keep this for myself. I made it up last night as soon as I found it in the box. Sorry." She blushed. "I tend to go on."

"Well, I'm with the girls. Wow," Payton echoed. "I can't wait to see what else you do. If you wouldn't mind showing me sometime?"

"Anytime, I'm glad you like them," Emily said, warmed by the reaction.

"Ready to go?" Quinn touched Emily's arm.

"You sure you can't stay for dinner?" Payton asked.

"We already have dinner plans," Quinn countered.

"You're taking Emily on a date?" Joy flowed from Jules.

"I am," Quinn answered and tweaked the end of the girl's nose.

Sara clapped her hands.

"What's this, you conspiring against me?" He reached out to tickle the younger girl.

"We like Emily. She's nice and pretty," Sara said in her ever openness.

"Well, I can't argue with that, because I think she's both those things, too. So that said, I'm going to take her to dinner. Without my matchmakers present."

"We could come," Sara wheedled.

"I think not squirt. I hopefully can handle this all on my own. Maybe some other time."

"A picnic?" Jules suggested getting into the conversation. "This week?"

'We'll see. Bye now." He winked, placing a hand on Emily's back as he reached around her to open the door.

"Bye," Emily got out.

"Sorry," Quinn said as they walked to the car. "I know those two. They were working it out in their heads how to get us to stay and I'd rather our first date be on our own."

ᴄᴙᴤ

First date, the pleasure the two words created in her lasted all through dinner as they talked about whatever came to their mind. She learned more of him and told of herself. Emily found a comfort she'd never really felt before. In college, she'd been too busy working and trying to graduate as quickly as possible, and still be one of the top in her class, to have much time to date.

After graduation, she'd been trying to prove herself and follow what was expected. Then there was Greg, and everyone convinced her they were the perfect couple, though she never felt it herself. Usually, she went along with everything he wanted, except for sleeping with him.

She smiled to herself as Quinn walked her to her door. Quinn was a gentleman. She liked that he opened doors. *Yes, she could do it herself, but it was nice being treated special.*

That was one of the things Greg never did for her. If anything, she was more apt to open the door for him. *No more thinking of Greg, He'd messed up too much of her life as it was, she was not going to let thoughts of him mess up this feeling.*

"Thank you for dinner. I had a really great time," she said as they approached her door.

"You think you might like to do it again sometime?" He took her hand as she turned to him on the doorstep.

"I'd like that." Emily was conscious of the strength in his fingers.

His free hand came up to caress her cheek.

Emily's senses explode with pleasure as her knees went weak. It was a simple touch, but never had she had a man touch her so. Never had a man's touch affected her like that. With a brief caress it seemed he claimed her heart for life.

Emily looked into his intriguing eyes. In the porchlight they flashed more gold. She wondered if he'd kiss her. She didn't kiss on the first date. *First date.* It really was just the first date. Her heart screamed she'd known him forever.

He leaned forward, then as if catching himself, he settled back. A smile crested his lips. "Goodnight, Emily." The back of his finger stroked her cheek again before lowering.

"Goodnight. Thank you for dinner." So breathless, she hardly got the words out.

He waited until she unlocked the door, then turned as she pushed it open.

He spun back at Emily's gasp.

Chapter Five

He saw no danger, but guessed her distress immediately. Quinn was at Emily's side, wrapping an arm around her and moving her behind him in a single protective movement.

The small kitchen would have been tidy – if cabinet doors weren't hanging open, drawers pulled out, and the contents of several dumped on the counter and table.

"Stay back." He eased into the room.

Instead of her remaining in the doorway, he felt her move with him. Her hand settled on his back, though she gave him space. The house she was renting was a cottage style, built around the same era as his house, but on a much smaller scale. Just inside and to the right of the door, a bow window held a small kitchen table with only two chairs.

On one side a curved archway led into a dining room. Quinn could see that another, much wider arch made the distinction from the living room. He figured the smaller opening, also curved following the theme in the house, went into the hallway to the bedrooms.

That's the direction he opted. He stopped first to check what he thought was the hall closet. What he found were boxes stacked on steps to the ceiling and realized it was actually the access to the attic. But, with the boxes completely blocking the way, he figured he didn't have to worry about checking up there.

The first bedroom he came to had obviously been converted into Emily's workroom. From the gasp he heard over his shoulder, once more, its disarray was not normal. He paused long enough to look in the closet, which since the doors stood open, made it easy to check. The bathroom only required a quick glance to tell it was clear and looked to be untouched before moving on.

A light breeze coming from an open window greeted them as they stepped into Emily's bedroom. It didn't show the same chaos as the kitchen and workroom, though the lid on her jewelry box stood open as did the small top drawer of her dresser. Quinn went to check the closet, then pulled out his phone.

It was only a moment before it was answered. "This is Quinn Lawson. I'd like to report a break in. I'm at … Emily what's your address? Emily?"

He turned to see her still standing in the doorway, her eyes wide with fright, and one hand covering her mouth.

"Emily." He stepped to her, reaching to take her hand. "I need your address."

She blinked, her chin quivering. She drew in a shaky breath, nodded and gave it.

Quinn repeated the address in the phone.

"Do you feel like you are in eminent danger?" the dispatcher asked.

"No. I'm sure whoever was here is gone. I don't know if our arriving here scared them away or if they left here before," he answered, sliding his arm around Emily. She leaned into him. He could feel the shivers that ran through her body.

"Is this your house?" The question came through the phone.

"No. A friend. I was just bringing her back from dinner."

"Can you stay with her?" the woman on the line asked. "I'll get someone there as soon as possible."

"I'll wait," he assured, disconnecting the call.

"The police are on their way, but I don't know how long until they'll get here," he said gently. "Why don't we go wait in the other room?"

She nodded, but before he could turn her, her arms wrapped around him and she buried her face into his shoulder.

Quinn enclosed her in his arms in response, pulling her tight. He felt the moisture of her tears dampen his shirt. "It'll be all right," he promised.

She nodded, but still clung to him for several minutes more before she eased back enough to get her hand up and wipe away the tears. "Sorry." She didn't look up at him.

Quinn brought a hand from around her to place under her chin, tipping it up. "It's okay. I'd be lying if I said my heart hadn't been pounding while going through the house. The tears are just a way to let off the tension."

That brought a little laugh from her. "And how do you release your tension?"

"I hold beautiful women and think of kissing them."

"Oh," the sound escaped her as her head came up, and her gaze met his. "And has that worked?" Her words came breathless.

"Let's see." Slowly, he lowered his head, giving her plenty time to pull back.

She didn't. Instead she stretched up and brushed her lips over his.

Quinn longed to tighten his hold, but the damp spot over his heart stilled his hand. Emily was frightened, vulnerable, and he was one man that would not take advantage of it. Still, he buried his fingers in her hair to steady her head as his lips settled more firmly. The touch of salt on her lips did nothing to dampen his desire.

When the kiss ended his heart was pounding for a whole other reason than it had been moments before when searching the house. He leaned his forehead down to rest against hers.

There was a moment of silence, then Emily broke it. “Well, how’d that work?”

The absurdity of the question, with the new kind of tension he was feeling, made a laugh burst from him. He pulled her tight, in a strong hug, then settled back. “Pretty good. Come on, let’s go wait in the living room for the police.”

His gaze darted around the room. He debated on closing the window, but decided to leave it until the police checked it out. The room had a soft, pleasing, what was considered country feel that was popular now, and fit Emily to a T. It also would fit in his house. The thought slipped in before he could stop it.

They’d only known each other for two days, he reminded himself as they walked down the hall. The problem was, it felt like he’d known her, or at least, been looking for her forever. Her living room held the same type of charm. Warm browns and cream, with touches of red, like the fluffy throw draped over the edge of the couch. It was a room a woman or a man could be comfortable in, cuddled up in front of the fireplace.

“I like your house,” Quinn said conversationally

“Thanks, it was one of the things that drew me to this area. When I saw it, I knew I was to come here.”

“I’m glad you did. So you’re not going to try to stay here longer or buy this place.”

“I wish I could.” She stopped and looked around. Her shoulder relaxed as an ease seemed to seep in her. “I’d buy it in an instant, but the couple that own it are gone somewhere in service for their church and will be back in three months, so that’s the longest I can stay. I really need to get looking, but it just hasn’t felt … right yet.”

Before he could comment, the doorknocker sounded. Quinn motioned her back and answered it, stepping aside to let a pair of policemen in. The first, Officer Thomas by his name tag, was a tall black man. The second to his surprise, was Officer Carlson who looked just as surprised to see them.

"Well, this is unexpected, Mr. Lawson." Carlson extended his hand then looked beyond him to Emily. "Miss London."

"Officer Carlson," Emily greeted. "You have the night shift today?"

"Just working over a couple hours so one of the guys could attend his daughter's birthday party."

"That was nice of you."

"We all help out. It looks like you've had some more problems." He turned to his partner. "I met Miss London –"

"Emily, please." She cut him off. "I know you about as much as I do most people in town."

"Emily." Carlson smiled at her. "Yesterday, someone tried to break into her car and assaulted her when she got in the way. How are you feeling, by the way?"

"Fine, no more headache."

Quinn saw the slight arching of Officer Thomas's eyebrow. The man didn't miss the significance of two attacks in two days, especially when you consider they were in what was considered a low crime area.

"Can you tell us what happened?" His voice was low and smooth.

Emily nodded. "I left about five and walked over to Mr. Lawson's to deliver something for his nieces." She glanced at Quinn. "He gave me a ride to their house so I could deliver them, then we went to dinner."

She swallowed. "He was just dropping me off. We went around to the backdoor because that's where the driveway is, and it has the motion-sensor light. When I opened the door, I saw drawers pulled out and some dumped." She was trembling visibly now so Quinn took over.

"We went through the house and didn't find anyone, but the bedroom window is open. The screen has been knocked out."

"Okay," Thomas said. "We'll take a look around. Did you touch anything?"

"Just the back doorknob and the one in the hall leading to the attic."

"Good. We'll be right back, then try to get some prints." Thomas stepped into the kitchen.

"Why don't you wait here?" Carlson suggested before he followed his partner.

After they did a sweep, they had Emily look around and see if anything was missing. Considering her TV and laptop were not touched, nor the sixty dollars sitting in plain sight on her workbench, while inches away her containers of supplies had clearly been searched. It tended to say robbery wasn't the motive.

"Do you know what someone would have been searching for?" Thomas asked.

Quinn glanced at her. He'd been wondering the same thing.

She shook her head.

"Have you had any other trouble before yesterday?" the officer continued.

"No. My life has been nice and quiet since arriving here."

"Arriving? How long have you been here?" Carlson joined the questioning, looking up from the small notebook he been writing in.

"A little over three months. This can't have anything to do with where I lived before. No one would care about me from then, I didn't even have any family there."

"What about your ex-fiancé?" Quinn couldn't help ask, but he really didn't want to know. He was starting to think the man was a fool for letting her get away. Then again, he didn't think her fiancé had ever taken the time to know her.

"No. He wouldn't take the effort. It would be," she paused, "beneath him."

"Miss London," Thomas said. "Whoever broke in here, didn't care you knew he was here. In fact, I'd say he wanted you to know. He didn't leave any prints, but, he didn't seem to take anything. For us, that is worrisome."

"What he's saying." Carlson stepped forward. "You need to use caution. Is there somewhere you can go tonight, or someone that can stay here with you, so you aren't alone? It might be for the best."

She shook her head. "Do you really think he'll come back tonight?" she asked.

The two officers exchanged looks.

Carlson is the one who spoke up. "I would say it's highly unlikely, but it's possible. We'll put in a request for drive-byes, but, I'm afraid that's the best we can do."

"Thank you. I appreciate it."

The men nodded and headed for the door.

"If there's anything else we can do." Thomas stopped at the door and handed her a business card.

"Thank you," she said again. She stood there a second before turning back to Quinn. "I can't thank you enough for being here."

"I could stay," Quinn volunteered. "Sleep on the couch."

She shook her head. "You wouldn't fit on my couch, it's nice but a little short. Besides, I'll be all right. You heard, they doubt he'll be back tonight, and they'll have a car in the area."

"That's no guarantee," he countered. "You could stay at my place. There are a lot of bedrooms. You could even have your own floor."

She laughed. "I'll lock up tight."

"I really can stay and help you clean up."

She stepped closer to him, reaching to cup his face. “That’s sweet, but no. Most of it will be separating and reorganizing, that’s something I’ll have to do myself. But, thank you for the offer.”

“You know, guys don’t like to be called sweet.” He laid his hands on her waist.

“I thought they didn’t like to be called nice.” She cocked her head to the side, and grinned.

He made a mock disgusted face. “Yeah, now, ‘my hero’ works.”

“Not, ‘brave handsome hunk’?” she teased.

He groaned. “We might be able to work with that.”

Emily laughed, feeling lighter inside. His gaze settled on her lips, and she became aware of how close they were standing, his hands sliding around her waist. Her insides did another shift as her heartbeat quickened. Drawing in a breath, she caught the enticing notes of wood and spice that combined into a masculine scent that was all too sexy. *Like Quinn Lawson needed any help in that area.*

His head dipped. The trembling started in her again. She wanted his kiss so much it frightened her. She didn’t know what to do or say.

He stopped a breath away from her lips and pulled back.

“Sorry, Emily, I’m rushing things. That wasn’t my intention. I didn’t mean to frighten you.” He let out a breath. “I just seem to forget we just met.”

“I’m not,” her decree was ruined by her voice quivering. She swallowed. “I’m not frightened, really.” Warmth burned through her and she knew her cheeks were turning a noticeable shade of pink. “I’m sorry. It’s …” She stumbled over the words. “I don’t usually kiss a man on the first date. Actually, I’ve never. In the bedroom … I …” Her words faded totally out.

His lips curved up slightly. “First date. Tell you what, to ease your sensibilities, why don’t we consider this the second date. We can count the cookies on the porch as the first."

At 'sensibility', all the apprehension in her faded. "Actually, I don't think I ever have on a second date before either." The playfulness returned in her.

"Okay, this is real good then. I'll consider myself special." He grinned. "But I guess this means it's too soon to ask you to marry me."

Now she laughed. He'd done it once again, flipped her emotions.

"Hey, legend has it my great-grandparents met over a distressful moment not unlike this one. He came to her rescue and it worked for them."

"Really, what happened?" Emily's insides shifted again to curious.

"I think I'll save that for our third date. That way I know you might let me have one, and since you won't let me stay, I best be going."

A touch of disappointment hit Emily at the thought of him leaving. Not because she was afraid to be alone, but because she really did like him being there. Unfortunately, he was right. She followed him to the door.

Leaning down, he brushed a kiss across her cheek. "Lock up after me," he instructed and waited for her nod. "I'll call you in the morning, but not too early in case you have trouble getting to sleep. Good night."

He took one step down when she stopped him. "Quinn."

He turned back.

Emily found herself almost eye to eye with him. Unwilling or able to stop herself, she leaned forward and pressed her lips to his. It was a brief kiss, there and gone, but it didn't make it any less powerful.

"Good night." She closed the door. Her heart thundering as she fumbled with the lock. Done, she pressed her hand to the wood. She knew he waited just on the other side until it was secured.

ଔଓ

Quinn had a hard time leaving, even after he heard the deadbolt slide home. His lips still felt the brief contact from hers. In his life he'd experienced his share of deep, passionate kisses, but never had one affected him as much as the brief taste of Emily. She was like coming home. Like it had been when he stepped into the family house after it had become his.

He wanted to knock and ask her to let him back in. *So it's too soon to ask you to marry me.* The teasing words had slipped out, but now said, they niggled at the back of his mind – like a glimpse of the future.

Quinn shook his head and walked to his car. What was getting into him? He didn't jump into things. He'd dated Charlotte for a year before he asked her to marry him, and look how that had turned out. He hadn't truly known her at all. Though, Charlotte had worked hard to put up a good front. He doubted he would have seen her true self until after they were married if he hadn't come upon her by chance.

His thoughts went back to that day. He'd just left a business meeting, when he noticed her having lunch with a friend, and gone to join them. His mind jumped to the scene. The two beautiful, elegantly-dressed women sat outside at a patio table of a stylish, popular restaurant.

He approached, weaving his way through the umbrellas that added atmosphere as much as shade. Overhearing the conversation as he approached, he stopped, shocked at what the woman he thought he was going to marry was saying.

Charlotte was looking at her engagement ring.

"Your ring is so beautiful," Charlotte's friend said.

He'd felt a stab of pleasure until he heard Charlotte answer. "It's okay, but I expected bigger. He can afford it.

After we're married, I'll have him get me something that I want."

Quinn missed what her friend said as he tried to wrap his head around what his fiancée was saying in a cool, dissatisfied tone. Charlotte's words were clear though. "Yeah, well, he also thinks we're going to live in this big, old house that is his grandfather's. It doesn't even have a pool."

"You can always put in a pool," her friend said.

"No. It's old." There was no missing the disgust.

"And you haven't told him?" her friend asked.

"Of course not. For some reason he loves the place."

Even from where he stood, he could see her nose wrinkle.

"He doesn't need to know until after we're married," Charlotte continued.

He'd stepped in then. "Actually, he did need to, and now he does, and a few other things." He turned and walked away.

A second later, he'd heard the clicking on tile as Charlotte came scurrying after him in her spiked heels.

"Quinn," she called in her cajoling voice that irritated him. "Darling."

When she caught his arm, Quinn was surprised at the speed the woman managed in her ridiculous shoes. He stopped and she moved around in front of him. "Darling."

Against his will, he'd looked at her, but didn't say anything.

"Where are you going?"

"Somewhere, where you are not. Maybe my old house, since you will never be there." He clenched his jaw.

"Now, darling, you misunderstood."

"I think it was pretty clear, even to as big a fool as I am." He shook his head in self-disgust. "I think I knew all along, I just didn't want to."

"No." She shifted in front of him when he tried to step around her, so he'd have to push her out of the way to go. "I was just bragging a little, you can understand that. Men do it all the time. A little one-upmanship."

"I don't. I always thought it was crude. Especially when regarding someone I cared for."

"Cared for," she spewed out. "See, you didn't say loved. You might care for me, but you don't love me."

"I guess that's correct, but did you even care for me, or was it always just my money? We're done. But don't worry, you can keep the ring, that's all you ever wanted. Though, I guess from what I just heard, you don't want it either. Still, it's yours."

His mind shifted back to the present and looked at the little cottage. He'd been such a fool. He hadn't loved Charlotte. He'd settled for the packaging and an act.

Climbing into his car, he started the ignition. Heading for home Quinn thought of the man that built the house. His great-grandfather. He would've been disappointed in his choice of Charlotte. Well, he wasn't going to make a mistake like that again. When he married, he wanted love, the true deep bond that lasted a lifetime.

Chapter Six

Stopping in the doorway to her workroom, Emily shuddered at the mess. Not one of her carefully organized containers remained intact.

What could the intruder have been searching for? Nothing was overly valuable. Most were bits and pieces that she'd gotten at estate and yard sales, like the box she'd purchased from Quinn's nieces. The thought of the girls brought Quinn right back to her mind, not that he'd been far from it since the moment she met him.

With a sigh, she closed the door and went down the hall to her room. She checked the window for a third time like she'd done with all the others in the house. Donning a pair of comfy gray pajama bottoms and an aqua T-shirt, she climbed onto her bed, but couldn't force herself to lay down.

A second later, she slid off the bed and dropped to her knees. She pulled the old box from under the bed where she'd pushed it the night before. She hadn't taken much time investigating the contents because she'd found the set of earrings and broken brooch for the girls' barrettes right on top, then seen the key she'd made into her necklace.

Leaving the box on the floor, she got up and went to the dresser. Picking up the necklace she'd taken off only a few minutes earlier, she fingered the old key. It truly was unique. She'd never seen one quite like it before.

Delicate intertwined hearts made up the bow of the key. Her first thought had been to do wire wrapped with crystals on it, but when she saw the words '*My greatest treasure',* embossed down the stem, couldn't bring herself to cover them. Emily wondered as she did the night before if it was the original key to the house.

Could the man that broke into her car have been searching for this key especially? He'd mentioned skeleton keys, but that made no sense. All the locks would have been updated. It would no longer work to get into the house. Besides, how would he have even known about it? No, it had to be something else, but what?

My greatest treasure. Quinn had said his great-grandfather called his wife that. She was surprised he'd gotten rid of the key, especially with the reverence he had for his history. Maybe he didn't know it was in the box. She'd return the key to him. It was the right thing to do.

That decided, she put the necklace down and returned to the bed and the box. She shifted thing around for a moment then realized there was a tray. Emily lifted it out to reveal the compartment underneath. "Oh," she let out, surprised at the find.

While the top tray held an assortment of discarded pieces of jewelry, the bottom compartment held the original items of the box. A pair of scissors in a scabbard, needles, a button hook, several thimbles, crochet hooks and spools of thread. All were easily fifty to a hundred years old. Valuable, maybe, but she didn't think it was worth breaking into her car or house for. She'd have to do some research, but not tonight.

Placing the tray back in the box, she closed the lid, and slid it back under her bed. This time when she settled back, she let out a sigh and her body relaxed. Tomorrow she'd do some research on antique sewing boxes and show Quinn the key.

A third date. Pleasure flowed through her at the thought. He said he'd call and she didn't doubt him.

He'd kissed her. Emily reached up to touch her lips. She'd kissed him. His taste seemed to linger. She closed her eyes, letting her mind flow over every detail.

ঙ৪৩

Quinn disconnected the phone call, leaned back in the chair and stretched. Business wise, he was done for the day. Glancing at the clock, he wondered if it was still too early to call Emily. It was almost ten, it should be okay. He'd been up almost four hours.

Something told him Emily would be an early riser, but he could be wrong. Had she been able to go to sleep or had worry kept her up? He should have stayed. She hadn't wanted him to, or if she had, she hadn't allowed herself to admit it.

The question was, would she feel like he was pressuring her if he called her so soon? She had been the one that came to his house the day before. Did that mean something? Like maybe she'd wanted to see him, or was her visit really just for the girls? He blew out a breath.

Since they were together, it had been easy enough to slide into dinner. It had made sense, and he'd already been planning on asking her out, but it was her coming there that instigated the date before he could. Their time together had been good. Better than good, until they found her house had been broken into. Concern surged in him. He picked up the phone.

Once more, the image of her looking up at him came to his mind. It was the picture of uncertain desire. Her tongue dampening her lips. Tasting him? He wondered if she even realized she'd made the intriguing little move.

The kisses had been a combination of awareness in them and a lot of other tension. He hoped she hadn't regretted them. He sure hadn't.

He brought up her number but before he could press call, the door chime sounded through the house. Leaving the phone on his desk, Quinn headed to answer the door. The thought that it might be Emily, like the day before, had him quickening his pace.

The silhouette of a man visible through the beveled glass squashed the possibility. The man in the designer three-piece suit was familiar, but he had to think to bring up his name.

"Mr. Raine," he greeted the attorney who handled his grandfather's estate. "Is there something wrong?" He didn't realize lawyers made house calls, unless it was billable.

If the man thought he might pull business his way, he was out of luck. His family's corporation already had a firm on retainer and was quite happy with them. The only reason he'd dealt with Raine on the estate, was Raine had taken over from his grandfather's old friend and attorney here in town after the man had retired.

"Oh, no, at least nothing with the estate." The man eased himself inside. "I'd just been at the police station. I do some pro bono on occasion. Anyway, I over-heard your name associated with a …" He tilted his head to the side as if questioning. "A break in. I was wondering if there was anything that was needed."

The offer took Quinn by surprise. He decided quickly the man truly was trying to drum up business. The problem was, there was something about Raine he just didn't like, something under the surface.

"Oh, no," Quinn assured. "Just a friend had her house broken into last night. There's nothing for you to be concerned. I had just taken her home. The police think it might be the same man that tried to break into her car the day before. They have a pretty good description of him, so it shouldn't be too long until they find him." Quinn hoped it was true.

"Well, if that's the case then I'll be off. If there is anything." He let the words hang.

"I'll let you know."

"Oh, and how did your niece's sale go?"

Quinn had forgotten the lawyer had been there when they were preparing for it. "Very well, thank you."

"They were so excited. Youth, and such a noble cause."

"Yes, they were quite excited." Quinn heard his phone ring. "Sorry, if you'll excuse me."

"Of course, I have to get back to the office. I just wanted to stop by to let you know I, or my firm, are available if needed."

"Thank you." Relieved, Quinn closed the door behind the man and ran for the den and his phone. By the time he reached it, the call had cut-off. Once again, it wasn't Emily, but this time he was more pleased to see the caller, and quickly redialed his sister.

"Morning. What's up?" he said in way of greeting.

"Sorry to disturb you," Payton apologized.

"You're not. In fact, you just saved me. Grandpa's attorney stopped by. You made a great excuse to get rid of him."

"Wasn't he at the house the day we were preparing for the yard sale? Wandering around, looking in things."

"Yeah, I remember. He wanted to see the house."

"I actually thought he might come back and buy something, but he didn't," Payton said

"I think he's just trying to wheedle business out of us. He hasn't seemed to grasp that the only reason he handled grandfather's estate was that he took over for Mr. Jenkins."

"What was his name?" she asked.

"Raine. Oliver Raine."

"That's it. There's something … I don't know … shifty, I guess you'd call it. I know that's not fair. He just seems too interested." She tried to brush her comment aside.

Quinn realized that was the same feeling he had. He was more used to people being interested in him for their own gain.

"So," Emily cut through his thought. "Why I called was, the girls have been bugging me all morning about when you're going to take them on that picnic, and I wondered, if perhaps, it could be today." She hesitated. "I could meet Richard for a late lunch. He has a big meeting with the contractor on the new phase this morning. He's been preparing for it for weeks and we haven't had much alone time," she cajoled.

Quinn laughed. "Let me see if Emily would like to join us. Either way, what time do you want me to pick up the girls?"

"You're awesome. How about around one? We just got done making cookies and I doubt they'll be hungry for a while."

"Sounds good, but I expect a bag of the cookies."

"That was one of the reasons we made them. I also have roast beef croissant sandwiches for you, potato salad, carrot sticks and apple slices."

"You didn't have to go to all that trouble. I could have just stopped and got something." Quinn settled on the edge of the desk.

"It's part of my bribery." She chuckled.

"It worked with just the cookies. I'll see you soon." He disconnected and now had an excuse to dial Emily's number.

"Hello," she answered on the second ring.

"How are you doing today?"

"Quinn. I'm fine. I've got everything cleaned up and back in their boxes and am just finishing up a plaque."

"So, does that mean you're too busy for a picnic or are going to be ahead enough to take a break? Looks like I'm babysitting with picnic plans."

Emily laughed, sounding like the cheerful woman that first caught his attention. Whatever stress she'd suffer the night before didn't seem to be haunting her now. "The girls are not going to let you out of it."

"Nope. So, want to join us? Otherwise, I'll just be asking you again later this week because they won't let you out of it either."

"I'd love to go for a picnic. What do I need to bring?"

"Just yourself. Payton's taken care of the food as bribery. Her word. She's planning a date with her husband."

"That's nice."

"I thought we'd go to the lake. There's a park there and some good hiking trails," he suggested, a touch uncertain what she'd think of that plan.

"Sounds good, I'll wear hiking shoes," she answered much the same way he had Payton.

"Great. I'll pick you up about twelve thirty and we'll go get the girls."

"I'll be ready. Bye."

Quinn found he didn't want to let her go which was silly because he'd be seeing her in two hours. "See you soon." He finally hung up.

With anticipation fueling a burst of energy, he decided to head to the attic and work on a little cleaning.

ଔ

Spurred by the knowledge she was going to see Quinn today, Emily dove into the next project she needed to get done. She finished it and another before it was time to get ready, which didn't take more than brushing her hair and changing her gym shoes for hiking boots. She already wore denim capris and a light blue athletic tee. She slipped on the key-necklace to show him and added a pair of stud earrings. Going into the kitchen, she heard a car pull into the drive.

She opened the door as he made it up the steps. “Hi.”

“Hi,” he greeted back. “Well, you look like you got enough sleep last night. No bad dreams?”

The blush snuck over her, but she managed to ignore it. “No, I slept fine.” *Fine. She dreamed of him kissing her.* At least that was when she awoke, and it was more than fine. “I just have to fill my water bottle and I’ll be ready to go.” She used that as an excuse to turn from him before he wondered about the heat in her cheeks.

“I forgot to grab one. Remind me to get one from Payton. I’m sure she’ll have one packed for the girls.”

“Here.” She reached into the cupboard, pulling out a second. “You can take the blue and I’ll take the lime green.” She put ice then water in the bottles before screwing on the lids.

“Thanks. Ready?”

Emily reached into the coat closet for her backpack, and dropped her purse inside with the water bottles. “All set.” He opened the door for her then waited for her to lock it, before leading her around the car to get that door for her, too.

The sun, the lake, the lunch, all were perfect. The girls were so excited when they got there. Sara had given her a hug and hadn’t let go of her until they got in the car.

“Mom, wouldn’t let me wear my barrette because she was afraid I’d lose it, but I wore it this morning. I love it,” Sara said in the way of greeting.

They laid out on the blanket Quinn had brought and stared at the fluffy clouds, picking out shapes.

“There’s a seahorse,” Sara pointed out.

“It’s more just a squiggly,” Jules said.

“You see what you see,” Sara defended.

"I think she got you there," Quinn said then added. "How about we take a hike now? There's a small waterfall not far up that way." He pointed to the trail.

Sara jumped up, catching his hand before he hardly finished speaking. "Come on." She pulled him along.

Emily stood, pulled on her backpack and reached out a hand for Jules. Together they walked along the path. On the way, Emily taught the girls camp songs while Quinn laughed and teased her. Emily was needling him about singing when they reached the waterfall.

"Oh, this is pretty," Emily exclaimed, taking in the water cascading over a ten-foot drop. A small pool formed at the bottom surrounding a sandbar, wildflowers and a few bushes, all nestled with a backdrop of tall pines.

"You haven't been here yet?" Quinn asked.

"No, I'm sad to say I haven't done much exploring outside of town. I've been busy setting myself up and am just starting to make friends. I know better than to hike alone."

"We'll have to do more then. There's a lot of places to see around here."

A thrill of anticipation surged through Emily. "I'd like that." Her voice was a little breathless, but if he noticed, he didn't comment on it.

They took off their shoes and waded in the water's edge, which blossomed into a water fight, girls against Quinn.

Water was dripping from his hair before he called for a stop. "I think we better try to dry off in the sun before we head back."

They settled back on the rock shelf.

"You know, you owe me a story." Emily looked at Quinn.

"A story!" Sara bounced closer to him.

"All right, but you may have already heard it. It's about my great-grandparents, your great-great-grandparents. This took place in 1929. Your great-grandmother, her name was Sarah, like yours." He reached over and tweaked the end of Sara's nose. "But with an 'h' on the end. You were named after her."

The little girl let out an "oh" and snuggled closer.

"Well Sarah's parents died, so she went to live with an aunt. Sarah worked as a seamstress. Do you know what that is?"

Sara shook her head but Jules nodded. "She sewed clothes."

"Correct," he said. "So Sarah moved to a new town to live with her aunt and took a job sewing. She was supposed to be very good at it and designed her own clothes. Sarah was also very beautiful. Fair, with blonde hair. Well, our great-grandfather, Ethan, saw her and was smitten, that means he was interested, but he was too nervous to approach her."

Quinn looked to Emily. "He wasn't the only one that noticed her. The banker in town was a wealthy, powerful man. I guess he liked to throw his position around. He set his attention on Sarah, but she didn't like him and when he asked her out, she turned him down. He became more persistent, and that scared her."

"She probably thought he was gross," Sara said.

Quinn smiled. "Probably. Not being a nice guy and was not used to being told no, he got mad. Well, one day when Sarah was leaving the shop where she worked, he waited in the alley for her. He tried to ask her out again and when she said no, he became violent. It just happened Ethan was walking home from work at that time and heard the struggle and her scream and came to her rescue."

"And he beat up the bad guy," Sara cut-in.

"He did. He took Sarah home and bright and early Monday morning went to the bank and took out all his money and cashed out all his investments, because the banker also handled the investments in town. Ethan said he wouldn't do business with someone that acted the way he did with a lady. That was September second, 1929. The day before the stock market hit an all-time high for the time period."

"Sarah and Ethan started dating and got engaged a couple weeks later and were married a month after that on October 18th. And, on the 24th something big happened in history. They call it Black Thursday. That was when the stock market crashed and a lot of people lost a lot or all their money."

"But, great-great-grandpa had taken his money out of the bank," Jules said.

"That's right. In fact, he'd taken it out when it was at the highest point so he made a lot of money and didn't lose any."

"Because he saved Sarah and wouldn't have anything to do with the bad man." Sara's head bobbed up and down knowingly.

"Right." Quinn said. "But, he said even more valuable than the wealth he received was getting Sarah. She was his greatest treasure."

"What happened to the bad guy?"

"Well, the story goes on, that he got most of his money first before there was, what they called, a run on the bank. But a lot of people lost all their money and had to sell their land. The price of property dropped because so many people were having to sell and no one could afford to buy. The banker was trying to buy up all the property at really low prices. When Ethan found out, he stepped in and helped some people save their land and bought the land at a fairer price from those who wanted to sell. He also put men to work, and there weren't many jobs at the time."

"That was the depression. We talked a little about it in school," Jules said.

"Yes. Your great-great grandfather was one person that came through it okay, he credited it to Sarah."

"I think it was because he was honorable and did the right thing." Emily commented. "You have a great heritage."

"We do," Quinn agreed, and the little girls' nodded their agreement.

"Was that who built your house?" Emily asked.

"Yes, for Sarah."

"That reminds me." She lifted off her necklace. "I think this confirms your story, I wonder if this might have been the original key to your house. It was the one I found in the sewing box. In fact, after your story, I wonder if the box might be Sarah's. We'll have to take a closer look at it. If it is, you should have it back."

"You bought it fair and square," he pointed out.

"Yeah, but if you didn't mean for it to be in the sale."

"I probably wouldn't have known what it was."

"Well, look at this." She held out the key, moving the other charms she'd added out of the way.

"My greatest treasure." He read. "You might be right. The key wards look a little too complex for the average house key though, especially for the old skeleton type. It might be for a cabinet or chest. It's not the key to the box you have?"

"No, way too long."

"I can see why you liked it. It's a cool key. I'm glad you made it into something personal." He reached out and slid the chain back over her head. His gaze met hers and held. Slowly, he lowered his head toward her, pulling back just an inch away when giggling erupted beside him.

"Okay you two." He gave his nieces a sour expression that made the girls erupt into full laughter. "Now, since we're mostly dry, I think it's time to go. Your mother's going to wonder what happened to us."

He stood, extending his hand down to Emily. "You two look away for a moment," he said when she placed her hand in his. He pulled her up and into his arms, capturing her mouth in one fluid move.

Warmth, not from the sun but no less intense, rushed over him. He really liked what kissing her did to him. He wanted to kiss her again but with the girls there, he pushed the longing down. “Okay, ready now.” Quinn took her hand and started walking, leaving all the females in stunned silence as they moved with him.

They were about back to the picnic area when Sara started to lag a little.

“Can I have a ride, Uncle Quinn?” she whimpered.

“I don’t know.” He drew the words out. “You’re getting big. I might not be able to lift you.”

“Pl-lease.”

He stopped, placing a hand on either side of her waist and made a mock effort to lift her, letting out a loud groan. Settling her back down, he groaned again, making her giggle.

“Uncle Quinn, I’m not too big.”

“You sure?”

She nodded.

“Okay, let’s try this again.” This time he wrapped an arm around her and lifted her, tucking her under his arm so she draped face down and headed down the trail with her laughing.

Emily pulled out her phone, opening to the camera and took a picture of the pair.

“No, a piggy back,” Sara squealed.

He stopped. “I’m not a piggy.” He dropped her feet to the ground, shifting to kneel in front of her so she could climb on. He rose, boosting her higher so she squealed again.

Emily took another picture, then turned to take one of Jules. The girl blushed, smiled and posed, then she made a silly face while Emily continued to take pictures. Emily laughed and switched to selfie mode and joined her. They were laughing when they broke from the trees and headed for Quinn's truck.

Emily was removing her day-pack when she caught sight of a man watching from a dozen cars away. Even at the distance of a hundred feet, she recognized the man immediately. Thinking fast, she raised her phone and snapped a picture before he could turn away.

"Quinn!" she pointed. "The man. It's him."

Chapter Seven

Quinn spun, needing no other explanation. “Stay with the girls,” he yelled as he took off after the man who was almost at the end of the parking lot.

“Stay close.” Emily pulled the girls to her side, wrapping an arm around them while shifting her phone’s camera to video.

Quinn had covered about half the distance when the man stopped running. A second later, Emily heard a motorcycle roar to life. Instead of the man driving back through the parking lot, he cut up one of the trails away from Quinn then along the tree-line back to the road.

Emily watched Quinn stop and stare after the disappearing motorcycle before turning to walk back to them.

“Emily, was that the man that tried to hurt you?” Jules asked.

Emily bent down opening her arms to encompass the girls to create a circle. “I think so. Your uncle was trying to see for sure.”

“But why would he be here?” Sara asked.

Emily felt a hand settle on her shoulder, but knew only comfort from the touch.

“Out of the mouth of babes,” Quinn said.

“I’m not a babe, Uncle Quinn.” Sara wrinkled her nose.

“I know, pumpkin. It’s just a saying and a wise one. It means you pointed out the right thing. How about you ladies get settled in the truck while I make a quick call?" He exchanged glances with Emily.

A minute later he got in. "Officer Carlson said he would swing by your place in about an hour and a half. He wants to tack this on to the other reports. He doesn't believe in coincidences either. So," he added more upbeat, "let's get you girls home."

Even seeing the man couldn't mar their time with the girls. That was evident when dropping them off, Sara ran into the house announcing that Uncle Quinn kissed Emily.

Payton arched an eyebrow. "Oh, he did. Interesting. What are you teaching my daughters?"

"I told them to look away," Quinn said in defense. "I can't help it if they peeked. Besides it's not like they haven't seen you and Richard kiss. You two do it all the time. I've seen you. So maybe you're the one who gave me ideas."

Payton just shook her head.

"Sorry. We have to go." Quinn grinned.

"Thanks." Payton gave them both a hug.

They were pulling into Emily's drive when Quinn's phone rang.

He connected with the hands-free. "Hello."

"Mr. Lawson. I'm sorry to bother you. This is Brenda at Mr. Raine's law office. When we were having you sign papers, I'm afraid we missed having you sign in one place. If you are at home, Mr. Raine was wondering if he could meet you at your place in about ten minutes. He has it with him. Unfortunately, it has to be now because he has to be back for an appointment."

"I'm not home right now, but I'm not far from there. Is there a way he can meet me at my location?"

"I'm afraid not. The reason he has the opportunity now is that he is driving right by your house on his way back to the office. He really needs that signature to finish up."

"All right, I'll be at my house in five minutes."

"Thank you so much. I appreciate it. I'll let him know."

Quinn disconnected and turned to Emily. "It looks like I have to go home for a minute. Would you like to come with me? We should only be about twenty minutes. We'll be back well before Carlson gets here, then maybe if you'd like we can do something tonight?"

"I think I'd like to wash-up. As for doing something, I have some chicken and vegetables. I was planning to make stir-fry. If you'd like to join me? I have plenty." The look of pleasure he gave her made her breath catch.

"That sounds wonderful. Maybe we can pick up a movie. I'm up to about anything, new or old. I'll admit, I'm kind of behind on the newer releases."

"I have a long back list I've been wanting to see."

"Great. You know, since we're having a break in the day, I think it qualifies as date number four. That's makes this the longest relationship I've had in months."

Laughing, Emily reached for the door handle.

"Hold it right there. This is a date. My mother would not approve if I didn't act like a gentleman." He came around to let her out. Helping her down, he pulled her into his arms and kissed her hard and deep before leaving her.

"See you in about twenty minutes." He waved as he drove off.

A few minutes later, Emily was in the bathroom running a brush through her hair when she heard a noise. She froze, looking to the door, telling herself that it was just the house settling. Still, feeling only slightly foolish, she reached over and carefully engaged the lock.

Pressing her ear to the door, she listened. No other sound reached her. She started to relax when she heard creak. After living there for over three months, she knew the sounds, and it was the floorboard between the spare bedroom and kitchen. Pulling her phone from her pocket, she activated the keypad punching 9-1-1, but stilled her hand before hitting call.

Surely, if Quinn returned, he would have knocked. He wouldn't have just come in. No other sounds reached her. She'd just about decided she truly was being foolish when she heard another sound, a scuff just on the other side of the door.

Pressing call, she listened both at the door and to the phone. Emily bit back a scream when she saw the door handle jiggle.

"What is your emergency?" The voice asked in her ear.

Emily gave the address. "There's someone in my house." She said in a low voice, looking around for some kind of a weapon, unfortunately, she pretty much kept the counter free of clutter. Her hand closed around a perfume bottle when something rammed against the door. She screamed as the door burst open. She dropped the phone and stumbled back, almost falling into the tub.

༄

Quinn pulled into his driveway followed by the urge to turn around and return to Emily. Never had a woman affected him so. It was like – like he'd met the piece of him he'd been searching for. The part he'd been hoping for when he asked Charlotte to marry him.

The only thing was that with Charlotte he'd been trying to force a bond that was never there. With Emily, it was just there. Sighing, he turned off the engine and climbed out. Raine should be there in two minutes if the man truly was on time. He shook his head. Once more he wondered what it was about the lawyer that irritated him so.

His aversion had been almost immediately, but came to a head the day he'd been trying to go through things with his nieces, gathering stuff for the yard sale. Raine showed up to sign papers. He had hung around, coaxing for a tour of the old house. Raine wandered around for about an hour, commenting about this and that.

Quinn could give him credit, he had done his homework. He knew a lot about the house and area history that tied with his family. Still, it was not going to get the lawyer the business he was obviously vying for. He just didn't like him.

Raine's sleek new sports car with an outrageous sticker-price pulled up in front. The man got out, heading toward him with a large toothy smile.

"Quinn, thank you so much for meeting me. I so appreciate it. I don't know how my secretary missed having this paper in the packet. She is usually so competent."

"No problem. If you have it for me, I'll sign it. I need to leave." Urgency surged in him.

"Of course." The lawyer came up the stairs, placed his briefcase on the table and opened it.

Quinn wanted to yell at him to hurry.

"Here it is." Oliver Raine pulled it out in a grand motion, laying it out, drawing a pen from his pocket, offering it over.

Quinn wanted to snatch the pen and just scrawl his signature, but growing up under the tutelage of his father and grandfather, took the time to read over the document before signing. The funny thing, he could have sworn he'd read the page before. Still, he signed, handing it back.

"I understand you have to get going. Thanks for bringing this by." Quinn headed down the stairs.

Raine was slow in following him. "I wanted to talk to you sometime about some estate planning. You have quite the heritage in this house alone to be protected now it is no longer under your grandfather's trust."

"I'll think about it and get back to you, but I'm afraid I have to leave now." Quinn kept going toward his truck.

"Of course. Have a good day," Raine said from behind him.

The man was still standing on the lawn where he'd left him when Quinn glanced back as he pulled away. For a man supposed to be rushing to an appointment, he didn't seem to be in much of a hurry.

ଓଃଧ

"Give me the key." The man held out his hand.

"Wh-what key?" Emily stammered. She recognized the shaggy hair and leather jacket. He was the one who broke into her car. "I don't know what you're talking about." She tried to stall for time for the police to get there.

"You lie again and you're dead. The one around your neck. I saw you show it to Lawson. I want the key and the chest," he demanded stepping forward. "Then I'll leave."

Emily could tell he was lying. He didn't even try to hide his face from her. "Chest?"

"The one from the sale." The words spewed with venom.

"The sewing kit?"

"Yeah, that thing," he snapped.

"It's in the bedroom."

He took another step forward, threateningly. "I searched the room."

Emily leaned on the counter as if edging back. "It's there. I'll show you, if you'll just leave."

"I said I would." The man growled and again she didn't believe him. "Show me!"

Stepping forward, Emily slid her hand across the counter snatching up her straightener, swinging it at his head. He blocked the move easily, as she knew he would, but was unprepared when she raised her other hand with the perfume bottle she'd palmed before he crashed in. She sprayed him right in the face.

It was only a small spray, but it caught him right in the eyes. He cried out, mostly out of surprise, but pulled back enough giving her the room she needed. She brought her knee up, ramming it into his groin. He went down, falling back into the hall. Unfortunately, blocking her escape to the front of the house.

Emily tried to dodge him as she sprang for the bedroom, but he caught her ankle. Tripping, Emily went down. She kicked back, catching him in the chin as much by accident as aim.

Still, his grip released her. She sprang up, sprinting for her room. Slamming the door, Emily locked it knowing it wouldn't hold, but once again it might buy her some time. She ran to the window, opening it and knocking out the screen that she'd just fixed that morning.

The bang at the door told her she didn't have the time to climb out. She dropped to the floor and slid under the bed just as the lock gave way, crashing back against the wall. Emily held her breath as the man stumbled in, going right to the window where the sound of sirens filtered in.

He cursed, climbing over the sill. He dropped into the bushes below and was gone.

Emily let out the breath she was holding. Turning her head, she looked over at the simple, antique sewing box that seemed to be at the root of all her trouble. She sagged, not as much in relief, but in curiosity. What was the man after? It didn't make sense, there had been nothing of valuable. She reached up and wrapped her hand around the key. There had to be more here than it seemed. When Quinn returned, they'd have to figure it out.

Quinn, just thinking his name had her wanting him. It was funny, in just a few days he'd taken up more of her thoughts and become more important to her than any other man she'd ever known.

Sirens crescendoed then fell silent, letting Emily know the police had reached her house. She slid from under the bed. Going down the hall, she stopped in the bathroom to pick up her phone.

"Are you still there?" she asked, not surprised her voice was shaky.

"Yes. Where are you?" the dispatcher asked.

"I'm going to the front door to let the officers in. He's gone."

"I'll hang up then."

"Thank you," Emily said as a knock sounded with the announcement of "police". Her fingers trembled as she unlocked the door. Tears threatened to spill over at the sight of the uniformed men. Funny, she hadn't felt nearly as shaky when facing the intruder.

ꕥ

Quinn fought the urge to speed, feeling foolish at his need to get back to Emily. It was hardly fifteen minutes since he'd left her. The sound of sirens drifted in through the open window, sending a shiver through him. "Just a coincidence," he said aloud.

The sirens cut off just as he turned onto her street. His unease swelled to fear. Ahead flashing red and blue lights blocked the street directly in front of Emily's house. *Emily*!

He punched the gas petal, then braked hard, skidding to a stop one house over from hers. Slamming the truck into park, he was out in a single motion, running for the door, calling her name.

An officer turned as if to stop him. At that moment, he heard his name and Emily flew from the house. They covered the ten feet between them in less than a second. He caught her as she dove into his arms. Trembling wracked her body as he tightened his hold and he held her as tears broke free.

"He was here," she stammered between gulps of air.

"Shh, it's okay." He tried to soothe, holding her to him. "It's all right. I'm here. The police are here. It's okay. I'm not going to let anything happen to you. Shh."

After a minute more, she drew in several shaky breaths and calmed.

"That's it." Quinn ran his hands up and down her back, comforting her a moment more until the two officers who had disappeared into the house stepped back out, coming toward them.

Quinn eased her back. “You okay?” When she nodded and swiped at the moisture on her cheek, he turned her to the officers.

“Ma’am, you made the call?” a tall, redheaded officer asked

“Yes.” Emily nodded. Her hand tightened on Quinn’s waist.

Before the officer could ask another question, a third police car pulled to a stop out front and Officers Carlson and Thomas got out and hurried toward them.

“Steve, what did you find?” Thomas asked.

“The intruder left before we got here. What’s up?” the red-headed officer answered.

“We were headed over here on a follow up with Miss Lawson, when the call went out. Fortunately, you were closer. Can you and Meyer do a sweep of the neighborhood and we’ll take the report?”

“Sure.” He motioned to his partner and the two went off.

Carlson turned to them. “Why don’t we go in the house and you can sit down?”

Emily nodded, but stayed tight to Quinn’s side as he walked her in. Settling her on the couch, he went to get her a glass of water.

From across the room he heard Thomas ask, “Can you tell us what happened?” The deep voice was smooth and comforting.

Emily’s voice was still shaky when she said, “Quinn had just dropped me off from a picnic with his nieces. We saw the guy.”

“We’ll get to that in a minute,” Carlson said. “Let’s do this now.”

Quinn wanted to thank the man. He needed to know what had transpired in the fifteen minutes he’d been gone to have the police here with lights flashing. Coming back, he settled next to her.

Emily's fingers were steadier as she took the glass. "Thank you." She sipped, then continued to work the glass around in her hands as she started her story. "I was in the bathroom brushing my hair."

Quinn went cold, the thought of Emily trapped by a man who had already assaulted her. When she said the man asked about the key, his gaze dropped to the innocent looking object, as she brought a hand up to wrap around it.

Surely, there had to be some kind of mistake, Quinn wanted to say, but kept quiet, stretching his arm out on the cushion behind her. It was just an old key. Any lock it went to would have been changed out decades ago. It had to be a different key. And better yet, if the key really was to something, how did the man know about it?

When Emily said he demanded the sewing box, Quinn's hand, resting on the back of the couch, clenched into the padding, his knuckles going white. Had the box of odds and ends that he thought of as junk, really put her life in danger? He didn't know what to think. One thing was certain, he wasn't going to let anything else happen to her.

Pushing the thought away, he focused on what she was saying, amazed at how resourceful and brave she'd been. She'd saved herself. He should have been there.

Which again was foolish, they'd just met each other. Even if they'd known each other for years, they couldn't be together all the time. Still, he wanted – more – needed to protect her. His mind was going in circles.

"Did he get the box?" Carlson's question brought him back.

She shook her head. "It's under my bed."

"I'd like to see it."

She started to stand.

Quinn shifted his hand to her shoulder, pressing her back down. “I’ll get it.” He needed a moment to collect himself.

Every bit of settling he managed on the way across the room shattered at the sight of the broken lock on the bathroom door. The hair straightener and a bottle of perfume lay on the floor where she’d dropped them in her struggle. Anger flared again. He barely got it tamped down when the broken door at her bedroom had his emotions surging once more.

She was okay, he said the words over in his mind. She was better than okay. She was amazing.

The window in the room once more sat open. Nothing else looked amiss. Getting down on his knees, Quinn looked under the bed, then stretched forward to reach the box.

Pulling it out, he really looked at it for the first time. It was so innocuous. True, as workmanship went, it was impressive. Made of walnut, the top had been inlaid, and the corners dove-tailed.

He wondered again how it had gotten in the sale pile. He knew he hadn’t placed it there, and the girls had been very good about asking him about items if he hadn’t already placed them in the pile to get rid of. Raising the lid, it really did look like useless junk. Except in Emily’s hands. The way she looked at the items gave him new appreciation for them. Reuse or remake. If the box really had been his great-grandmother’s, he knew the woman would approve of Emily.

Closing the lid, he picked up the box and headed back to the living room.

Emily was still going over details of her story. He waited until Carlson looked at him before he came forward, setting the box on an antique trunk she used as an entertainment table.

"You got this from Mr. Lawson's sale?" Thomas asked.

"Yes."

"May I ask you what drew you to purchase it?" the officer wondered.

"The first thing." She lifted the lid. "All the pieces of jewelry and watches. But the box is incredibly beautiful, too. I would have probably looked at it, but I was focused on its contents. I really did get the better end of the deal." She glanced at Quinn and smiled for the first time since he'd gotten there.

If they'd been alone, he would have argued with the statement. His heart was telling him that he had. But, it had nothing to do with the transaction, and all with the woman it led into his life. Quinn could swear Emily blushed, turning her eyes back to the box.

Carlson reached out and picked up several pieces, fingering them before putting them back down. "So none of this is valuable?"

"Not that I've noticed. I haven't really looked at it all yet. But, it all seems to be old costume pieces, most broken," she answered.

"And the key doesn't go to the box?" Officer Thomas asked.

"No." Emily shook her head. "It would've looked similar to this key, but been smaller. The stem …" When the man looked confused, she lifted the key around her neck. "This area." She pointed to the long part of the key. "It's called a stem, shaft or shank. So the one for the box would have been much shorter. This one is actually quite long, and the wards here at the end, the part that turn the locking mechanism, are very intricate. This key really is a work of art."

"And the key was in the box?" This time it was Carlson that asked.

"Yes, I saw several others in there, but none like this one. It's the reason I haven't explored the box more. I normally would have, when I first got home. But, I found it right off and stopped my search to make this necklace, and a couple barrettes for Quinn's nieces. I promised them."

"Do you mind if I look at that?" Thomas motioned to her necklace.

"Not at all." She slid it over her head and handed it to the officer.

"What's this engraving? My greatest treasure."

"It actually goes back to how my great-grandfather referred to his wife," Quinn put in.

Thomas arched a brow. "I'm surprised you would get rid of it."

"I actually didn't know it was in the box. In fact, I didn't even know of its existence," Quinn answered.

"So if you'd known, it wouldn't have been in there?" Carlson asked.

"Honestly. No. But Emily bought it, so …" He shrugged.

"I was going to give it back to him, but he refused," Emily said quickly, coming to his defense.

Quinn wanted to kiss her. Okay, it seemed like he always wanted to kiss her. She was just so sweet and caring.

Both officers grinned before returning their attention to the box. Thomas laid the necklace down and picked up several pieces, studying them. They all joined in, laying the items out on the trunk, in categories of jewelry, watches, keys and even several old tokens and a couple of Indianhead pennies and a buffalo nickel.

Emily looked at Quinn. "I really do owe you more for this box than I paid."

"How about we add a couple more homemade dinners on it," he said forgetting for an instant the two officers were there. "Sorry," he said to the men.

Thomas seemed to find humor in it. “Quite all right, I totally understand. As my grandmother would say, you’d be a fool if you weren’t interested.”

Quinn laughed.

Emily blushed and turned her attention to lifting out the tray that Quinn hadn’t even realized topped the box until they started taking the stuff out.

“So this really was a sewing kit and not a jewelry box,” Carlson said, looking at the items still in the interior.

“Yes.” She studied it in the bright light coming in through the window. “And by the care, and that it’s complete, obviously well used, I would say it was a prized possession. I told Quinn, I haven’t done any research yet, but I would bet it is seventy-five to a hundred years old. Maybe even more. It’s in amazing shape though. Especially, having the scissors and thimble that I think may be original. Sorry, I didn’t mean to go on.”

She glanced around at the men. “It does make it more valuable. I don’t really know yet. I’ve never bought one before. Never really had the opportunity. I think collectors usually scoop them up and I can’t afford collector pieces for what I usually do.”

The men joined her in studying the box.

“A couple hundred dollars usually doesn’t illicit multiple break-ins.” Carlson pushed the other keys in the grouping around then picked up the one on the necklace, fingering it a minute before putting it back down. “Okay.” He sat back. “Why don’t you tell us about this afternoon?”

At Emily’s glance his way, he got that she wanted him to take the lead on this. “I took Emily and my nieces on a picnic to the lake. We hung out at the park then went for a hike. We were there a good three hours. We just made it back to the truck when Emily saw him. He was a ways down the parking lot and took off when I headed toward him. He hopped on his motorcycle, rode up a trail, along the side hill to the road.”

"Giving credence that he was watching you," Thomas said grimly.

"I thought so."

"Can you add to the description?" Carlson leaned in again.

"I have a video of him," Emily spoke up.

"You do?" Thomas asked.

She nodded. "I don't know how clear it is. I haven't had time to check it out yet. Not sure I wanted to, but I took it when Quinn was trying to catch him." Emily extended her phone, which she'd been fiddling with, laid it on the table and pushed play.

Both officers sat forward along with Quinn. It clearly showed Quinn in pursuit of the man at the other end of the lot. Unfortunately, the man's back was to her.

"You're certain this was the same man?" Carlson asked.

"Yes. Positive," Emily said just before the man stopped and turned, mounting his bike, giving them a good side view.

Carlson reached down, backed up the video, playing it forward again, stopping and enlarging the image. Even at the distance, the man's face was clear. "This may be good enough to run. Can I send this to my phone?"

"Yes, of course."

He picked up the phone and in the process the screen moved back a picture. "Oops, sorry."

Emily took the phone to bring up the video, then gasped.

Chapter Eight

Quinn reacted, sitting forward to look at the picture of her and Jules making funny faces at the camera. His muscles tensed as he wrapped his arms around her, drawing her against his firm chest. Emily burrowed in, trying to blank out the image of the figure standing in the trees, behind them. Though in the shadows, there was no doubt of the man in the leather jacket and where his gaze was focused.

Carlson took the phone, enlarging the image. "I think this eliminates any doubt it was a chance encounter. I want to warn you. This is more concerning than the break-ins."

When he stopped talking, Thomas took over. "This guy's following you. Watching you. The first attack could have been by chance. He didn't expect you back at the car. The second, you weren't home. But this, today, he was watching you. We have to figure he left the park, then came here and waited. Waited until you were alone. He came in the house knowing you would be here. He's escalating his game, and he didn't care that you got a good look at him."

"We'll put an APB, all-points bulletin, on him." Carlson started again. "Every law enforcement officer will be watching for him. We'll get him, but in the meantime, you have to be careful. It would be better if you're not alone."

"She won't be." Quinn tightened his hold. His promise echoing in her ear.

Suddenly chilled to the bone, Emily was grateful for his warmth and strength. At that moment, she felt more shattered than she ever had in her life. She was hardly aware of Officer Carlson sending himself the files or anything else they said until they stood.

"We'll let you know if there are any updates. If there is anything you think of, anything you see that concerns you, please feel free to call either myself or Officer Thomas." Carlson stood.

Quinn brought her up with him and kept his arm around her as they walked the officers to the door.

"Thank you." Emily found her voice. Just the moving around grounded her.

"You're welcome. Try to relax," Thomas said in his deep, rumbling voice. "We'll get the guy. We'll also keep a car in the neighborhood."

"I'm taking Emily to my house. I have a good security system and will keep an eye on her."

"That would be for the best," Thomas acknowledged with a nod. "We'll be in touch." With that, the two men left.

Quinn closed the door and locked it after them, then turned, pulling her tight against him. His chin came down to rest on her head.

Emily pressed her face into his neck, taking in his comfort and strength, feeling sheltered. She didn't know how long they stood there in the entryway with Quinn's hand sliding up and down her back but finally the shivers in her faded along with her fear. Emily managed to draw in a deep breath and let it out slowly. The next breath she took brought another reaction from her as she registered the spicy, masculine scent that was Quinn. Her body went from cold to hot in an instant.

"I'm okay now." Her lips brushed his neck as she talked.

She felt a shudder go through him in answer. He leaned back, raising his hand to her cheek, tilting her face up. Emily became lost in his gaze as his head dipped and his lips covered hers. She gave over all residual fears, registering only Quinn.

When the kiss ended, he tilted his head down to meet hers, so they rested forehead to forehead. "You know lady, you pack quite a wallop."

The absurdity of the comment shocked a laugh from her. "Sorry, I'm afraid that's all you. The guys I've ever dated usually said I'm old-fashioned at the best and a prude at other times."

"My ex said I was a cold hunk of stone," he countered.

"She didn't know you."

"No, she didn't, but then again, I don't think she was meant to." He kissed her again. "Come on, let's gather up the chicken and vegetables and anything else you need for the night."

At that, she pulled back. "Night?"

"Emily, I meant what I told the officers. I'm not leaving you alone. My house has a state of the art security system. No one's getting in there unknown. Don't worry, I'm not pressing for any more than your safety. I understood what you said about waiting in your relationship. If you haven't noticed, I'm kind of old-fashioned myself. So no sleeping together until we're married." He grinned at the comment. "You can have the whole second floor to yourself." His case presented, he stared down at her, waiting, letting her make her decision.

After a second of internal debate, she realized she felt good about the decisions. "I'll pack a bag. I'd like to take the chest."

"I think that's a good idea. I'll put everything back in while you pack."

She left his arms then turned back. "Quinn, thank you." With that she headed to her room. Emotions of a whole different kind washed over Emily. Never had she had anyone stand up for her like Quinn was. Sure, she'd had great friends growing up, but when she'd hit college they'd faded away. After that, she'd been so focused on her goals she hadn't forged any deep bonds.

Getting settled in the corporate world had been the same, working long hours, going home exhausted, only to redo it the next day. Shallow relationships with colleagues. That was how she let herself be drawn-in by Greg. She'd been lonely and looking for more.

And, that was the reason she'd left it all behind, not because of a broken heart. Her heart hadn't been broken or even bruised, it had never been involved. She had faced the fact she was not becoming the woman she wanted to be.

Thinking of the man in the living room and her feelings growing for him, she assessed how he fit in her life. Once again, the warmth of rightness flowed through her. It was too soon, she tried to tell herself, but it didn't seem to matter. She was falling in love with Quinn Lawson. And, for some odd reason, it didn't frighten her. If anything, it felt – right."

She blew out a long breath and pulled a duffle bag from her closet. It didn't take long to throw a change of clothes in the bag. She looked at her pajamas. Nothing frilly or sexy resided in her wardrobe of nightwear.

What she had was best describe as a light T-shirt and shorts made of a soft comfortable fabric. Pretty much the same thing she'd been wearing to sleep in since high school. She'd never needed to move past the style because no one, but her roommates in college which were all girls, had seen her in them. Not that Quinn was going to see them. Emily reminded herself.

In the bathroom, she grabbed her brush and small toiletry kit. That didn't take much time to pack either because she didn't wear much makeup. Even in her corporate days, she hadn't bothered with much. She could never see how it made her look any better and it took time she usually didn't have. Now, she just didn't worry about it.

From the way he talked, she'd bet Quinn's ex-fiancée wore expertly applied makeup, beautiful designer clothes and the filmy provocative nightwear. *Stop it!* She wasn't going to compare herself to a woman in his past. If Quinn liked her then he'd have to take her how she was, because she was never going to try to be someone else again.

Steeling herself, she headed back down the hall.

Quinn stood in the kitchen at the open refrigerator door. Emily's heart did a little jump, just like it did the first moment she'd seen him. It did another when he turned and looked at her.

"I'm not sure what vegetables you wanted." He stepped back as she placed her bag on the counter and came forward, but he didn't move completely aside. Emily couldn't help but be aware of his height or the width of his shoulders. She caught the spicy, woodsy scent she associated with him and forgot for a second what she was doing.

Forcing herself to focus, she pulled vegetables from the crisper. "Do you have honey?" she asked over her shoulder.

"Yes, and soy sauce, so you won't need it."

She looked back. "You like to cook?"

"I like to eat," he said simply, then added. "I've been a bachelor a long time. You can only mooch so many meals. Restaurants are nice to go out to, but are boring to eat at all the time by yourself."

Emily nodded, totally understanding. Even cooking for one was preferable to eating alone in a restaurant with couples and families surrounding you.

His lips tilted up in a grin, which accentuated the intriguing dimple in his cheek. "I think I'm going to hold you to those extra home cooked meals for the sewing kit and those old pennies."

"Oh, and how many meals are we talking about?"

"Hmm." He seemed to think. "I'm thinking one for each penny, at least two or three for the nickel."

"I don't think they're worth that much," she pointed out.

"I'll buy the supplies and assist."

"Okay, that might be sufficient. What about the sewing kit?"

"I'll have to think more about it." His eyes dropped to her lips.

Emily's breath caught at the intensity that burned in them. She could swear she saw the promise of a future there, then he stepped back.

"We better get going. I'm hungry." His gaze dropped back to her lips before he turned away. "I'll put your bag in the truck then come back for the sewing box." He snagged her bag and disappeared out the door before she could formulate a reply.

What was happening to her? Emily knew the answer as soon as the question crossed her mind. She truly was falling in love. There was no doubt about it.

Chapter Nine

What was happening to him? The thought hit Quinn as he headed to the truck and the answer was obvious, he was falling for Emily. And the thing was, he wasn't worried about it. Never could he imagine anything feeling so right. Patience, he yelled at himself.

He couldn't rush her. He definitely didn't want to frighten her away. He had to quit teasing her about marrying him. When he did ask, he wanted her to take it seriously, and believe that was truly what he meant and wanted for the rest of his life. But for now, he needed to concentrate on keeping her safe so they could possibly have a future.

He looked around. Nothing of concern showed. Still, he tossed her bag in the truck and elected to pull it into her driveway, so it would be just out the door. Maybe he was being a touch paranoid, but he could almost swear he was being watched.

The sooner he got Emily home the better.

Ten minutes later, carrying Emily's duffle and a small cooler while she carried the sewing box, they walked through the breezeway to his door. "Welcome." He stood back after getting the door open, letting her precede him in. He sat the cooler on the mudroom's bench.

"Which would you like to do first, get settled or dinner?"

"You did say something about being hungry."

"Yeah, but I can wait. How long will it take to fix?"

She gave a little shrug. "About twenty minutes. Fast and easy."

"Okay, let's get you settled first. This way." They dropped the cooler and sewing kit off on the kitchen counter before he led her down the hall toward the front of the house to the main staircase.

"This is so beautiful."

"I think you said that the last time you were here."

"But it's true."

"I'm glad you like it. Are you ready to see your room?" He took her hand leading her up the stairs.

"May I have a full tour later?"

"Of course, it would be my pleasure. In fact, if you have some suggestions I would love your opinion."

"My suggestion? The house is finished." She swung her arm out in an encompassing sweep.

"I know. And I did have some input when it was remodeled, but my mother didn't do all the bedrooms, and I've been thinking about changing a few things to put my own touch on it." He shrugged.

"And you want my opinion?" she asked confused.

"Just thoughts. All right?"

It was her turn to shrug. "Okay."

At the top of the stairs, they turned to the right. He stopped in front of the second door on the left. "This one or the next one are the rooms I would suggest. This one I call the white room."

He opened the door, and Emily knew why. White walls, sheer white curtains with a puffy white duvet, dominated the room, but wasn't overwhelming because of the black metal frame of the bed. White, black, gray and a touch of aqua accented the pillows piled on it. Above the bed, pictures of botanical drawings were set in white-washed frames. The room held a bright, airy, charming feel.

"This is the room Payton used when she visited before her house was built. The next one down is a more traditional room with a massive four poster bed. I'm afraid you might feel lost in it, but are welcome to use it. It's the one my parents use when they are in town because it has its own bath. The others have a connecting bathroom between them. These two both have fresh linens. The two on the other side of the hall, to the front of the house, haven't been updated yet. Though if you want, they are available."

"How many bedrooms are there?"

"Eight. The two rooms on the end have two twin beds each for children. The master suite and sitting room take up most of the other wing. There's a maid's room across from the kitchen. That's where I'll sleep tonight."

She spun to him. "The maid's room? Why?"

"I promised you the whole second floor," he said simply.

"But … I'm not going to kick you out of your room."

"Emily, it's no big deal. I've stayed down there before. In fact, it's where I stayed when I was fixing up my room."

"But, I don't want to put you out of your room." She took a step to him.

He placed his hands on her upper arms, his eyes intense as he looked at her. "I want you safe."

"I don't need to force you out of your room to feel safe here, and I think a whole wing is enough for me." A smile accompanied the warmth she felt. She raised up and brushed her lips against his cheek, then settled back, arching her eyebrow. Emily could see him give in.

"If you're certain. I'll be at the other end of the hall if you need me."

"I'm certain, and I like this room. It has a good feel. I think after everything, I need the brightness of it."

"You're amazing." He leaned down and brushed her cheek with his lips, but ended lip to lip for a second before he pulled back. “Come on. Let’s go make dinner, then I’ll give you the full tour.”

Fixing dinner was as pleasurable as eating it, which they did in the sunroom that extended out on one side of the house. With windows on three sides, the room was filled with light and nature. A fireplace made it so it would be comfortable all year long. Emily fell in love with it immediately.

Stomach filled, she relaxed, sitting back in the cushions. “Oh my,” she said contently. “I think I’m in love with your house.”

“Oh, you are?” He stood and moved to sit by her, laying his arm around her shoulder.

Without thought, she leaned into his side. “Yes.”

“Some people think of it as old.”

“But that is part of its charm, what makes it so special.”

He placed a finger under her chin to keep her gaze on him. “You do have a way of seeing the beauty in things.”

“Thank you. I’m afraid I lost that for a while, but I feel better about myself now. I might never run a major corporation, but I’m happy.”

“That’s all that counts.”

“It is.” She rested her head on his shoulder, snuggling in.

He wrapped his other arm around her. They sat like that, in comfortable silence, as the setting sun sent shafts of amber, oranges, and reds to fill the room with a golden glow.

“So what are your dreams for the future?” he asked while his fingers played with the strands of her hair.

“I’m pretty happy with how my business is going. I want to keep it up, maybe expand it. I’ll have to see how I feel about that in the future. My biggest pleasure is doing the work and seeing how it develops. Not every piece turns out the way I envisioned, sometimes I have to tear it apart and start again from the beginning."

"Kind of like your life?" He brushed a kiss across her temple.

"Yes, like the dragon fly symbolizes." She lifted the necklace to show the dragonfly charm next to the key. "Remaking or recreating ourselves."

"And do you sometimes see yourself recreating yourself into a wife and mother?"

Warmth flowed through her as Emily imagined herself holding a baby in her arms and reading to a little boy that looked way too much like Quinn. She started to push the image away then looked up into his eyes and it firmed.

"I dream of it now, with the right man."

The golds and greens in his eyes intensified as he studied her. Then his lips settled on hers and Emily felt her life remake itself in love.

The kiss continued, becoming more passionate. They were both breathing hard when they parted. "I could stay like this forever, but I don't think it's a wise move right now in our relationship." He raised a hand to brush her cheek. "I want a future with you, Emily. I don't want to rush you, or frighten you, but I want a future." His low gravelly tone testified of the words.

Emily felt the promise and the answer inside her. "Yes," she whispered the word, meaning it with all her heart.

"Yes," he repeated and kissed her hard, broke and stood, reaching out to pull her up. "So we have two options. I can give you the tour of the house now or we can wait until morning, when you can see it in the daylight, and we watch a movie tonight."

Emily looked around the sunroom. It still had charm, but she missed the sun streaming through it. "I really want to explore your house … but, I think I would like to see it in daylight. Do you have a movie in mind?"

"Do you like action adventure or comedy?"

"There's one I've been wanting to see that is both, if we can find it." She looked hopeful.

"Let's go see."

Holding hands, they went to the family room where they located the movie and settled on the couch to watch. They broke once in the middle to make popcorn, then snuggled down to finish.

"That was good," Emily said with a laugh.

"Agreed. I think I need to do this more often." He slid his fingers through her hair

"Watch movies?"

"With a beautiful woman," he clarified.

"Thank you," she accepted the compliment. "Didn't your ex like movies?"

"She was more into fancy dinners, parties and being seen."

"That doesn't sound much like you."

He winced. "That should have been my clue right there. I just didn't want to acknowledge it at the time. I let my male ego get in the way."

"How'd you meet?"

"A charity fundraiser my family always attends. She seemed interesting and interested. I was flattered and thought because of her family she wouldn't be attracted to me just for money." He grimaced again. "I was wrong."

She sat forward and looked back at him. "This house. You said you inherited from your grandfather, but I thought you were in construction."

"I am. The story I told the girls about my great-grandfather, it's all true. My family has been in construction since. Over the years, we've developed a lot of the land he purchased back then, and we've purchased other property along the way. Both my grandfather and my father have made wise investment decisions."

"So this house isn't just a part of your history that you're working to sustain?" Her chest tightened, making it hard to breathe.

"I am. Emily, I thought you understood. When we went to Payton's."

"Her house was the first in the subdivision. Her husband designed it and he works for your company. I guess I just didn't put it all together. You don't just build, you own it all?"

"Yeah. At least, our family does." He shrugged. "But, I've done it all, from pouring concrete to laying shingles. My father thought it was important that I learn from the ground up. I spent my summers in high school doing grunt work, then after graduating in construction management, I spent another five years working incognito at different sights to get a good feel of the operation."

"That's impressive."

"My father did the same thing. I figured it seemed to work for him." He looked away until she laid a hand on his arm.

"So what was your favorite thing to do?"

"Kind of like the whole thing, especially seeing how it develops. I don't spend as much time at sites any more. The last couple years, I've moved up to take some of the pressure off my father. We now pretty much team manage it."

"That's nice. So you don't swing a hammer anymore?" She took his hand turning it over, noticing the calluses there.

He closed his fingers around hers. "Every once in a while. I told you, I kind of like it. You can understand that."

She nodded. "I can. To make something. See it come together as you imagine."

"Yes." He raised his free hand to her cheek, cradling it as he came in for a kiss.

At the touch of his lips, Emily could imagine a wild array of possibilities, and they all led to a future with him. A whimper escaped her. He eased back, his fingers stroking her cheek, eliciting little shivers from her.

"We better call it a night."

She nodded, standing with him. Emily took the popcorn bowl into the kitchen while he turned off the TV, then picked up their glasses and followed her.

"I like your kitchen, actually this whole room is great."

He laughed. "Is there anything you don't like in my house?"

Emily wrinkled her nose and looked around. "Hmm, not really anything I've seen yet, but I'll let you know. I do have a couple accent pieces that you might like."

"Really, you'll have to show me."

They headed down the hall together. "I do have one thing," she exclaimed.

"What's that?"

"Keeping it clean. This must take a lot of work."

He laughed again. "Well, where it's just me, I don't make a big mess. "I'll admit, though, I have a maid that comes in every other week."

"Okay, I guess that's reasonable."

They stopped outside the door to her room.

Emily shifted side to side. Her heartbeat quickened as he stared down at her like he was drinking her in with an unquenchable thirst.

"Goodnight, Emily. Sleep well." With that he swept in for a quick, breath-stealing kiss that left Emily so stunned he was half way down the hall before she realized.

"Goodnight," she whispered after him. To her surprised he turned and winked before stepping into his room. Emily wasn't sure how she managed to open the door and make it in her room.

She'd heard of being kissed senseless but thought that was a myth. Kisses that she'd experienced had been nice but none had ever rocked her world. Her world had been rocked tonight.

A few minutes later, she laid back in bed, her mind going over everything of the day. The funny thing was, she felt no fear. All she could think of was Quinn Lawson.

❧

Quinn stretched out on his bed. His fingers interlocked behind his head, his thoughts on the woman down the hall. How could she mean this much to him after just three days? It might be crazy but it felt awful good. Was this what his great-grandfather felt when he met his greatest treasure?

Were they looking after him? Were they the ones that led him to Emily? He smiled at the thought. He didn't consider himself a romantic, but he was feeling like one blessed man.

❧

"What d'ya want?" the man in the black leather jacket snapped as he turned to face the man that stepped out of the shadows.

"To know what you think you're doing." Irritation sounded just as strong in his voice.

"What you wanted me to do."

"No. You've blown this from the start. All you were supposed to do was buy a chest of junk."

"That's right, you said junk. How was I to know someone else would want it? What's so important about it and some old key anyway?" He sneered. "They don't even use those anymore."

"That's none of your business. Your job was to get it, which you've failed to do. Now every officer in the area is looking for you."

The man in the leather jacket scoffed. "That's a joke. They'll never pin it on me."

"The Lawson name carries clout and the multiple attacks are causing a lot of concern. Top that, the woman was able to take your picture. They're running them now, along with an APB. They're taking this serious."

The man's head jerked up. "If they catch me, you'll just have to get me off."

"You threatened to kill her. You should have just done it." His tone was even colder than the man's in the leather jacket.

"Lawson was coming back. There wasn't time. I didn't think you wanted blood." He shifted uneasily.

"I want that key and the box." He ground out the words.

"I'll get it. It's just going to cost you a bit more if I have to kill someone and disappear so the cops don't find me." As soon as the man in the leather jacket met the other man's gaze, he knew his words had been a mistake. He reached for the gun at his back but wasn't fast enough, as the man brought his hand from his pocket. Moonlight winked off the barrel a split second before the shot came followed by a second.

The twin punches knocked the man back. His chest erupted in agony as he dropped to the ground, gasping for breath that he couldn't seem to draw in. He was aware of the man stepping forward to stand over him.

"You forget, I know you. Why couldn't you have done as you were told? I would have had the key and the map. Now, I'll have to get them on my own, and you'll still be dead."

With that the man extended his arm again and his world ended.

Chapter Ten

"I can't believe you make crepes." Quinn reached around Emily to snitch a raspberry.

"They're not hard."

He leaned against the counter watching her move the pan around to spread the batter. "Payton's going to want you to teach her how. She loves crepes."

"Anytime."

"My parents are coming to town in two weeks, any chance I can talk you into making breakfast while they're here?" He didn't mention that if the police hadn't caught the guy after her, she might still be there. He really liked having her around. It felt so …right.

"Sure, but you haven't had them yet."

"We'll just say I have faith."

"Well, you're about to find out. We're all ready to eat." She slid the last crepe on to the plate.

They each picked up a tray and headed for the breakfast room which, like the sunroom, jutted out from the house and had windows on three sides. Emily filled a crepe with berries and whipped cream, then rolled it up and sprinkled powdered sugar over the top.

"Wow," Quinn exclaimed after taking a bite. "This is a good way to start the morning."

"I didn't ask if you had work to do today."

"Nothing pressing. I have a few figures to go over, but I have plenty of time for your tour.

They started their tour in the kitchen, putting their dishes in the dishwasher. Emily loved the huge island and the whole layout, but her favorite thing was the pantry. With two entrances, the pantry ran the width of the kitchen, behind the stove and counter area.

"This has to be the most ingenious pantry I've ever seen."

"Thank you. I wish I could take the credit, but I'm afraid it was another Payton idea. We just knocked the wall out between what used to be the butler pantry and the food pantry. I don't know why it wasn't like this in the first place. It makes so much sense and is a lot more practical than having one pantry for table-linens and serving dishes and another for food, how it originally was."

"That's how it used to be done," she said in way of explanation.

"The same with the grand formal dining room and living room. I hardly ever use them. I spend most of my time in the kitchen, family room, den, and now, the sunroom. I admit, I'll go a week without going into the other two rooms," Quinn said as they walked through the formal living room that looked like it came right out of a magazine layout of the rich and famous.

"You don't entertain?"

"I haven't yet. I wasn't settled in here for Thanksgiving or Christmas. I'll probably get roped into one of them this year. And, they're already planning the Fourth of July here I think, unless I convince them that the pool at Payton's house is a better idea."

"I can't believe you have an elevator in your house," Emily said a second later, as they rode up to the second floor.

"I use it so infrequently I tend to forget about it. We put it in for my grandfather. He took a bad fall riding a horse about twelve years ago. He was in his late seventies.

It left him with a limp and made stairs hard for him, but he didn't want to move out of the house."

"I can't blame him. It was his family home."

"Yeah, so we put in the elevator." He motioned her to proceed him out as the doors opened.

"That's impressive."

"It wasn't as difficult as it sounds." Quinn shrugged it off. "While we were at it, we turned his room into a master suite. That was what started the updates. We took out a bedroom next to the master, enlarged the bath, and made a sitting room. Putting in an elevator worked right in. He'd been grumbling for years about redoing the bedroom and bath. He said they were fine, but he admitted he loved it when we finished. I think he liked the spa tub we put in as much as the elevator."

They stepped into the master bedroom and Emily could see why the man loved it.

"I changed the furnishings. He went for more old fashion, a very large padded, kind of an art deco headboard and dressers to match. He also wanted wallpaper like my grandmother liked. So the first thing I did was strip it off. The bed is just as big and bulky but more me."

"It's beautiful," she admired. The four poster bed had large carved columns of rich wood and a scrolled metal canopy. "You even make your bed," she said impressed.

"My mother wouldn't have it any other way."

Emily turned looking at the room. "I think you were right about getting rid of the wallpaper, but it probably still looked okay. But this …" The cream walls set a warm, relaxing atmosphere to the room. To the side, an arched alcove held the sitting area, and French doors opened onto a private balcony. "This is nice," she said stepping out

"Summer evenings under the stars and moonlight."

"Very romantic." She grinned back at him.

"Or a stress reliever. My grandfather loved to sit out here, read or just look out over the woods." Quinn walked to the railing and took a stance similar to how Emily imagined his grandfather or great-grandfather doing.

She watched him a minute until he turned to face her. "I like it."

"Me too, but wait until you see the bathroom. That was all my mother and Payton. Nothing to change there."

Emily followed him, then stopped in the doorway of the room, and had to agree. "This is magnificent. I bet your grandfather loved it. What's not too?" The cream walls continued in with the warm wood. The long marble counter with twin sinks was bordered by cabinets and an arch with recessed lights. The shower had multiple heads and could hold several people. Tub sat at the end of the room framed by the window behind.

"You know I think I better quit showing you my house. I'm afraid you might marry me for it," he said teasingly, but she turned to him in all seriousness.

"I love your house, but I promise you, when I marry it will be because I love you with all my heart."

There was no mistaking the intensity behind the promise. He also wondered if she realized she said "I love you". Quinn couldn't not act on it. He wrapped his arms around her and kissed her. There was no hesitation in her returning his affection.

Breaking, he blew out a breath, tilting his forehead down to rest against hers, in what was becoming a familiar position. "You know we probably shouldn't be kissing in my room." He stepped back, letting his hands fall. "So you have a decision. We can head up to the attic and I'll show you all the stuff in storage there, or we go outside for a few minutes and I'll show you something my great-grandfather built for my great-grandmother."

She bit her lip in thought. "Both sound appealing, but honestly, if I get in the attic I might not want to come out for a while."

"Walk it is. Let's go." He held out his hand to her and she took it.

They took the stairs and out onto the back patio. "I have to admit," he started. "I haven't been out here yet this year." He led her to a path that went into the woods. "There's approximately thirty acres here. It was part of the original homestead. The old cabin that was built in the late 1880s was a little ways over there. It's not standing anymore. It was gone before my time, but my grandfather showed me where it was. Told me the stories he knew."

"I hope they're written down."

"I'm not sure. I haven't found them yet if they are. But you're right, if they're not, I need to, even if it's just what I remember." After about ten minutes he slowed his pace.

"Is there something wrong?"

"I just didn't realize how overgrown it had become." He stopped in the middle of a small clearing, by a couple yellow and pink wild-rose bushes. He reached out fingering one delicate blossom. "I guess this was her favorite flower."

When Emily drew closer, she realized there was a stone bench that faced the rose bushes, and they bordered a boulder with lettering carved in it. She went forward and knelt down.

My greatest treasure,
My greatest love,
You hold my heart forever.

"Oh," she exclaimed as she ran her finger over the lettering. "How sweet."

"It is said she was sitting on this rock when he asked her to marry him." Quinn started to pull some of the weeds away.

Without a word, Emily joined him until he caught her hand. "We better wait and come back when we have gloves and tools. I just wanted to show you."

"I'm glad you did." She gave his fingers a squeeze.

They headed back to the house still holding hands.

"How about I fix us lunch while you get some work done?" Emily said as they entered the house ten minutes later.

"You don't need to, I can help."

"I'm keeping you from your work."

"I'm not complaining. Besides as I told you, I don't have much I have to take care of today."

She arched her brow and might as well said, "oh really", but didn't voice it.

He laughed. "I'll tell you what, we compromise. How about we do lunch together, then I show you the rest of the upstairs and the attic? I'll leave you there to explore to your heart's content."

"You trust me doing that?"

"I do, and I was kind of hoping I could talk you into helping me catalog what's up there. So I know what I'm looking at."

"Quinn, I'm not an appraiser."

"But you have a good eye and know a lot more than I do. I didn't even know that chest was a sewing box." When she hesitated, he continued. "You know what is worth keeping. There's almost a century of stuff up there. You know the thoughts of the depression era … keep, reuse. You never know what you might need. I'll pay you to help me go through it."

"You're letting me stay here," she pointed out.

"I'm doing that as a friend."

"And I'll do this as a friend."

It was his turn to hesitate. "Okay, settled," he said, then before she could turn, eased closer. "Emily, I'm also doing this because I care … a lot."

Her breath caught and she got lost in his amazing eyes as the gold burned in them. Placing a hand on his arm, she rose up to press her lips to his. When his arms closed around her, she wanted to stay forever, but the ring of his phone pulled him away.

She had lunch ready before he disconnected.

"Sorry," he said as he put the phone down and walked toward her.

"It's okay, let's eat." This time, they went out back to sit on the patio and enjoy the fresh air before heading inside and upstairs.

The afternoon flew by. They went through the other bedrooms. Quinn showed her the ones he was thinking of remodeling. Emily had to agree with him, though none were real bad, they definitely could use some updating. Especially the wallpaper. Emily had to laugh, his grandmother truly did favor the heavy intricate patterns.

They finally made it to the attic, and as Emily predicted, she became lost in the intriguing treasure trove. Quinn was not kidding at the amount. There was nearly a century of items piled there. So with a notebook and pen that Quinn fetched for her, Emily dove in while he went to his den to work.

"You have dust on your cheek," Quinn said, making her jump and drop her pen.

Emily placed a hand over her heart, trying to still its thundering. "No scaring your volunteer to death."

He just laughed and came over to sit by her. "How's it going?"

She stretched. "How long has it been?"

"About four hours." He winced. "Sorry, a couple led to more in-depth phone calls than I planned and a couple more things to handle."

"No problem. I haven't even finished this corner." She swung her arm around behind her. "There are some real nice things, some stuff I'd say just get rid of, and some things that could really be cool again. No journals or pictures yet."

"Okay, so you've been listing it all there?" He pointed to the book.

She nodded. "You know, if you have some sticky notes it might help to label things. That would make it faster when you're looking at it later."

"Sounds like a good idea. I have some in the den. For now though, how about we get out of the house and do some work of a different kind?"

"A little gardening?" she asked.

"That's what I was thinking. Actually, you don't have to help. You could just sit on the bench and keep me company if you'd like."

"I'm not bad at trimming if you happen to have a pair of gloves."

"I can probably find some, but you really don't have to. I think you've done your share of work for the day." He wiped at the smudge on her cheek. "I didn't bring you here to work you."

"I know, but I have to have something to do or I'll go crazy."

"We could bring some of your stuff over so you can work on it here."

"How long do you plan on me staying?"

"As long as necessary. At least, until the police catch this guy." He wondered what she'd say if he told her he was hoping she liked being with him so much that she'd want to stay forever.

"I need to go to my house and grab another change of clothes."

"Okay, how about we spend about a half hour weeding, then we'll swing by your place then grab dinner," he suggested.

"Works for me."

It actually turned out to be a little longer before they had the rose bushes trimmed, and all the weeds cleared out from around the bottom of them and the boulder.

"Much better." Emily stood back admiring their work.

"I'd say that's good for now," he agreed.

"We can probably get around the bench done tomorrow."

"Or later this week. There's no hurry."

ଓଃ

Emily tensed, unlocking her kitchen door. Nothing looked disturbed as she stepped over the threshold. Still, she was glad Quinn was with her and found it sad she'd lost the comfort of being in the little house. It had been such a perfect place to rediscover herself.

"So what would you like me too get?" Quinn laid a hand on her shoulder, giving a squeeze as if he knew she needed the contact.

"Nothing really. It will only take me a moment."

"You sure you don't want to bring some of your beads or other projects to work on?"

"I think your attic will keep me plenty busy."

"I don't want it to take up all your time," he said concerned.

"I'm not worried about it, besides it's interesting, and I'm hoping for first dibs on anything you wish to get rid of. Especially if there is any more jewelry pieces."

"Yours."

"Good, because I saw a couple lamps I think I might want. I haven't made my way over to them yet."

"Just let me know." He followed her down the hall. "I'll come over here tomorrow and fix these doors." He stopped to inspect the one to the bathroom."

"I'd appreciate the help. I need to get them done before I move."

"It's the least I can do. I feel bad that it happened, especially since it seems linked to me."

She turned on him, dropping the shirt she was about to put in her bag. "You are not responsible."

He smiled. "Yes, momma bear."

She relaxed her shoulders. "Sorry." She swallowed hard. "I just don't want to think you're spending time with me because of some sense of responsibility."

He left the door to stand in front of her, placing his hands on her waist. "Trust me that is not the reason. I like being with you. It feels good to be with you. Feels right."

"That's how I feel." She leaned into him and his arms closed around her. "It's all moving so fast."

His cheek brushed her hair as he nodded. "I've never had it be like this with any other woman. I've had flashes of desire at seeing a beautiful woman, but that's all it usually is, and burns off fast, but with you …" He tilted her face up to look at him.

He brushed his thumb over her cheek. "The moment I saw you, you caught my interest, but it's more. I enjoy being with you, want to be with you." He paused, drawing in a deep breath. "I envision being with you in the future. I've never done that with another woman, picture them with me as I grow old."

Emily's heart thundered. All she could do was nod until she swallowed down the emotion swelling within her. "I think I'm falling for you." The pleasure that filled his face took her breath.

He kissed her, nuzzling across her chin, pulling her into a tight hug. "It's good to know we're on equal footing." Before he could finish the sentence, there was a knock at the door. He ignored it. "Because the last two days that's what …" The knock came again this time louder, commanding his attention. "It sounds urgent."

"The police." Emily's thoughts jumped. "Do you think they found him?" Hope surged through her, making her dash for the door.

Quinn followed behind, his long stride letting him keep her in view when she opened it.

The tall, fashionably-dressed man was unfamiliar to him, but obviously not to Emily. The anticipation she'd showed seconds before had disappeared, replaced by what looked like stunned shock.

Chapter Eleven

"Greg." Emily stared at her ex-fiancé. "What are you doing here?" she demanded as she pushed down the instinct to shut the door in his face. Only schooling herself to be civil kept the door open. After all, it was her fault she'd gotten engaged with the jerk.

"There you are. I thought I had gotten the wrong address. You don't know how much trouble I went through to find you." Her ex-fiancé pushed passed her in to the house without waiting or being asked.

He stopped just inside the door and glared at Quinn. "Who are you?" He wrinkled his nose.

"He's a friend," Emily stated, putting herself between them. "And I would like you to leave."

"Darling." He drew the word out. "We need to talk."

"No. We don't."

Greg frowned, shooting a glare at Quinn before looking back at her. "Will you get rid of him? I came to apologize."

"Quinn stays. You can leave. I don't want or need your apology. I think everything was clear six months ago when it ended."

Greg stepped closer, but fortunately didn't reach for her because Emily was afraid she'd deck him.

"Look, darling, I know what I did was stupid. I was a fool. I accept that now, but I can't get you out of my mind. I broke it off with Kristy. She's gone."

"In other words, she figured out what you're really like and left. What, did you sleep around on her, too?" As soon as she said it, Emily knew she was right. "You can leave, now." She stepped toward the door.

"Now, darling, that's not it at all. Nothing is the same without you. I'll grovel if that's what you want. I talked to the other members of the board, and they've agreed to take you back, with a promotion and a nice returning bonus. You can start immediately."

"Do not call me 'darling'." Emily's hands clinched into fists, then she got an odd feeling. "Is that what this is about? Me coming back to the firm?" She stiffened on saying the words.

"No, of course not. When I let it be known I was coming after you, regret was expressed at letting you go. Several of your accounts have been struggling with you gone."

"So faced with the odds that they were going to lose them, they now want me back." She shook her head. "And with the bottom dollar at risk, you're willing to put up the show again."

"That's not it at all. I really do miss you. I miss having you to talk to. I didn't realize what a bright spot you were in my life. Everything was better. What can I say? Do?"

This time Emily felt some sincerity, but it wasn't near enough, not even if she hadn't met Quinn. It wouldn't have changed, because she had. "There's nothing. See, Greg, I realized it was as much a lie on my side as yours. Yes, you betrayed me, then turned vindictive and blamed me for your actions. I don't know how you can ever believe I would want you back. I could never trust you again. You shattered any caring I had for you."

"Caring. Not love," he snapped back. "You never loved me."

"You're right," Emily admitted. "I never really did. I know that now, but I was willing to give myself to you. I would have been faithful to you, cared for you and done everything to make it work. We probably would have been fine."

"Fine?"

"Yes, come on, that's all you wanted. The image. The status. You never loved me either, or you wouldn't have been sleeping with my secretary. But see, I let caring and hope for a future sway me, so I was willing to settle, believing it was what I wanted, too."

She didn't need to look at Quinn to feel him. "But now, I'm not going to settle. I want trust. But more, I want love. I'm not trying to be mean, but I want the joy of being with a man that holds my heart."

Greg looked over her shoulder at Quinn, then back to her. "And that's him?" He looked at Quinn once more.

This time she followed his gaze. Emily didn't say yes, but could've. She wanted Quinn and would forever. If it was him walking away, she would be shattered.

"That's it then?" Greg said.

She nodded, shifting back to Greg. "I wish you luck."

He glanced at Quinn again and turned away. In the doorway he paused. "I really was a fool, but you never looked at me like that. Good luck, Emily." He saluted her and walked out.

Emily watched him go, feeling a touch of sorrow, but no hurt. Turning, she met Quinn's gaze and her heart swelled.

"Sorry," she said.

"It's okay."

"Thanks for not stepping in."

"I figured you could handle it," he said easily. "You really never did love him."

She shook her head. "No, we were friends though. I realize that now, but he was right." Emily felt like she was on a precipice.

"How?" he coaxed, taking a step toward her.

"I never looked at him or any other man the way I look at you. I look at you and all I see – all I feel is … I love you."

"And I love you." Quinn opened his arms and Emily went into them. He just held her.

"So what do we do?" Her head rested against his chest, taking pleasure in his heartbeat.

"Take it as it comes. Don't fight it but don't rush it."

"One day at a time, just like me staying with you?" She tilted her head to the side to look up at him.

"Well, hopefully, a little different. I'm hoping the danger to you will be a very short time. Us, I'm hoping forever."

"Forever sounds good, if it's with you." Warmth flowed over her.

He kissed her. "We're getting pretty good at this. Come on, let's go home."

"One thing." She held him in place. "Will you promise to never call me darling?"

Laughter boiled out of him. "Promise." Taking her hand, he kissed her knuckles leading her out.

☙❧

Quinn put down the papers he was going over and glanced at the clock. It was about time to drag Emily out of the attic and see if she'd like to escape the house with him for a while. The chime of the doorbell detoured him from the staircase to the door.

"Officer Carlson," he greeted the man, opening the door wider to allow him and another man, who was dressed in khakis and a polo-shirt, to enter.

"Mr. Lawson." Carlson shook his hand. "This is Detective Hall."

"Detective." Quinn extended his hand.

"We need to talk to you and Miss London. Is she here with you by chance?" Detective Hall asked. He was of average height. A middle-age man with dark circles under his eyes that looked like they hadn't had much sleep in the last twenty-four hours.

"She's up in the attic. If you'd like to have a seat, I'll run up and get her." He led them into the living room, then headed up the stairs to the attic.

"Emily, I need you downstairs," Quinn said from the doorway.

She looked up from the box she was going through. Her brows wrinkled, but she put the books she held back in the box and stood. "What's wrong?"

"Nothing. Officer Carlson's here with a detective."

"You think it's about the man after me? That they got him?"

"I hope so. Let's go see." He caught her hand, keeping it firmly in his as they reached the bottom of the stairs and entered the living room.

"Officer Carlson." Emily looked from him to the other man.

"Detective Martin Hall, Ma'am." The man nodded to her.

"Emily, please." She sat on the sofa facing the men and Quinn settled down beside her.

"Officers Carlson and Thomas have gone over the incident reports with me about the man that broke into your house and attacked you. I have a few questions, if you don't mind?" Detective Hall asked.

"Then you haven't caught him yet." Emily sagged slightly. "I'd hoped." Her hands came up to cover her mouth and she blinked a couple times.

Quinn slid his arm around her waist and she leaned into him.

"We'll get to that," Hall said sitting forward. "Have you had any contact with the man since the break in at your house?"

"No." She shook her head. "I … Quinn let me stay in one of his guest rooms since. Except a trip over to my place the day before yesterday so I could get some more clothes, we've been here and I haven't seen anyone."

"Did you go on your own?"

"No, with Quinn." She looked to him and he nodded.

Quinn edge forward. "Is there something wrong?"

"No, I just had to ask. Also, can you tell me about what time that was?" Hall made a note on a small pad in his hand.

"About five-thirty," Quinn answered for her.

"And when did you get home?" Hall looked between them.

"About an hour later," Emily said. "We were planning to go out to eat, but an old acquaintance stopped by. Actually, to be clear, it was my ex-fiancé, and we decided to bring the food home instead because I didn't feel like going out."

"And during the day what did you do?" Hall asked.

"Just hung out here," Emily answered.

"The whole day?" Hall pressed.

She nodded.

"After the day before, I figured it was best to stay close to the house." Quinn put in.

"May I asked what you did?" Hall probed.

Quinn wanted to say not what you're probably thinking, but kept to the facts. "I gave Emily a tour of the house, then she worked in the attic. She's helping me catalog stuff up there. I worked in the den. Twice we took a walk out back to get some fresh air."

"And you were together?" Hall stressed, looking between them.

"Yes." Quinn studied the man. "I didn't want Emily alone after what's been happening. I've had the security system on the whole time."

The man looked up from his notebook. "Does it log times of activation and deactivation?"

"Yes," Quinn felt more puzzled than ever. He was beginning to feel like it was an interrogation.

"May I get a copy of that before I go?"

Quinn looked between the two lawmen. Carlson sat oddly quiet. "Can I ask what this is all about?"

"I wanted to verify your whereabouts. Officer Carlson and Officer Thomas both spoke in yours and Miss London's behalf, but I still had to satisfy myself."

"What's wrong?" Emily's voice cracked.

"Miss London, you don't need to worry about Sammy Wallace anymore." The detective took up a graver tone. "That's the man we identified as after you."

"You caught him." Emily slumped with relief, but after the questions, Quinn didn't feel it.

"Actually, no. His body was found early this morning," the detective said, his gaze shifting between them.

"Body? As in dead?" She shuddered.

Quinn pulled her tighter to his side. "That's what the questions were. Establishing our alibis."

"Yes, as I said, both Officer Carlson and Thomas spoke up for you, but I still had to cover it. I'd appreciate it if you could give me the security log though for my record. It would be useful."

"I can do that. Can you tell us what happen to Wallace? I'm getting the feeling he just didn't die of natural causes." Quinn's unease rose.

The detective paused, pursed his lips, then said, "Wallace's body was found by a jogger and his dog early this morning. In Woodland Park. Off the path in the trees. The dog found it, and when his owner went after the dog, he saw the body and called it in. Wallace's body had been dragged into the trees and left there. He'd been shot three times. Twice in the chest, once in the head."

Emily paled. "Do you know … no that's why … you were wondering if I did it?" Her voice trembled.

"No, actually I didn't suspect you, but I have to be thorough. Especially since he was involved in an open case against you," Hall explained. "Wallace wasn't a real nice individual. Not as bad as some, but he had a lengthy arrest record. Mostly B and E."

"Breaking and entering." Carlson spoke for the first time.

Emily nodded.

"He also had a couple arrests for assaults and an armed robbery, but was able to plead it down and only serve a year," the detective added.

"Only a year?" Emily's shock mirrored Quinn's.

"How long has he been out?" Quinn asked.

"Two months. He'd been keeping it clean as far as we can tell, except for you." Hall tipped his notebook toward Emily. "We don't know what set him off on you. It's not his style. He was the type that would do the job and move on."

"But, he didn't get the box or the key," Quinn pointed out.

"And that's a puzzle. Why he would want it so bad. I looked at his arrest records. He usually stole the normal things that were easily hawked. This box, especially coming back for it, doesn't make sense."

"If he just got out of prison, how would he even know about it?" Quinn asked the question that had been bothering him all along. "I didn't even know about it. Or at least, what it was."

"I've gone over that with Carlson and Thomas. They say it's a sewing kit?" Hall raised a brow.

"Sewing box really," Emily corrected. "They were quite common. This one is nice. It was well cared for. Sewing boxes were really personal to a woman. Like her purse but maybe more so. They often kept their most personal items there. Poems, love letters." Emily blushed and glanced at Quinn. "I read up on them last night before bed."

"And value?" Hall asked.

"Fifty to maybe a hundred and fifty. All depending on what you could get the collector to pay. Actually, the thread spools, thimbles and scissors are more valuable than it is." Emily explained.

"And you got all for forty bucks?" Hall asked.

"Yes, I got the better end, but I didn't know about the sewing stuff when I bought it. I wanted the pieces of jewelry."

"The broken pieces?" Hall glanced up from the note he was making.

"Yes." She nodded

"I know the officers already looked at the box, but I'd like to have a look at it if I may? I don't know what it could have to do with Wallace's murder, but his actions with you is what stands out as unusual in the last days of his life. Seeing as he was killed just a couple hours after threatening to kill you –"

"Couple hours." Quinn stiffened. "I thought you said you found the body this morning?"

"That was when it was discovered, but the coroner estimates he'd been dead for at least thirty-six hours. Making it possible that you were the last person to see him alive except for his killer."

Emily sucked in air. Quinn turned her, pressing her face into his neck, running his hands up and down her back as she shivered.

"I'm okay," she said after a minute.

"Good," Hall said gently. "Can we go look at the sewing box now?"

"It's in my den. I'll get it. With everything that was happening we didn't want to leave it at her house." Quinn stood.

"Is there a better place to lay it all out?" Carlson spoke up.

"Good idea," Quinn said. "Let's move in to the kitchen counter."

They waited as he retrieved the box then followed him into the kitchen area, where they settled in the breakfast nook instead and started once more laying out everything.

"That's it?" The detective looked puzzled.

Quinn and Emily both nodded.

"I thought you said it was used for personal items also?"

Emily looked thoughtful. "Quinn, you said she was a seamstress, but ..." Emily pressed down on the padded lining at the bottom of the box then ran her finger along the edge. Getting her fingernail under the slight lip, she lifted it up. It came easily, revealing a small stack of folded yellow-papers underneath.

"Oh." Emily looked up at Quinn before she reached in and reverently lifted the papers out. "The first letter seems to be written to herself. Like a diary page. The next several letters appear to be love letters to Sarah from Ethan." Emily looked at Quinn. "Your great-grandparents. "There are several other letters."

"That still doesn't sound like something Wallace would be interested in," Carlson said looking at Hall.

The detective looked over the items on the table and pursed his lips. "It doesn't make sense." He picked up one of the letters and held it to the light, studying the page until moving on to the next. He was shaking his head before he laid it down. "It doesn't make sense at all. Why would he be interested in this?"

"And, how had he known about it?" Quinn restated the question he'd brought up earlier.

The detective shook his head, and stood. "I don't know what to think, but thank you for talking to me. If I can get that security log."

Together they moved into the den. Quinn logged on to the system and printed the last three days, handing the paper to the detective.

"Thank you," Hall said as they walked to the door. "We'll be in touch, but please contact me if you think or find anything that might help."

"We will," Quinn assured for both of them.

They shook hands. Quinn shut the door and set the security system as was becoming habit. He turned to Emily and opened his arms. She stepped into him which seemed to be another habit, but a much more pleasurable one.

"It's over. He's gone," she said softly, as if she was trying to wrap her mind around the fact. "I wouldn't have wished him dead."

"But I'm glad he's not after you anymore," Quinn finished for her.

She nodded and leaned back. "At least, you can get rid of your house guest." She tried to add a hint of cheer.

"I kind of like my house guest." He tipped up her chin and kissed her.

"Well, I promise to come visit. After all, I still have an attic to go through. Oh, that reminds me I found a box with some old photos in it. A couple are tintypes."

"I'll have to take a look, but later. How about we fix dinner."

ꕥ

"You know, you can stay another night if you want?" Quinn said as they turned onto her street.

"That's the third time you've said that." Emily grinned at him. "I'll be all right."

"I know you will, but I'll still worry. And more, I'll miss you. I like having you around."

"I like being with you, too. I'm trying to remember we are trying to take our time."

"Now that's something I can't argue with." He glanced over at her as they reached her house.

"I don't think we were arguing." She smiled.

"True, I'm not much of an arguer." He wrinkled his nose. "Unless you're a contractor that won't get the job right."

Her smile turned into a laugh. "That's good to know."

Emily waited for him to come around and get her door. He grabbed her bag then started up the stairs beside her. They both froze at the sight of the broken window on her back door.

Chapter Twelve

"Not again." Quinn's comment echoed how Emily felt. He hustled her down the steps, tossed her bag in the truck and hoisted her in. Slamming the door, he pulled his phone out as he went around to the other side.

"Detective Hall, this is Quinn Lawson. I'm with Emily London outside her house. There's been another break in. I don't know if this is something you wanted us to contact you about." He listened a minute. "Yes. We'll wait out front."

He disconnected and started the truck, putting it in reverse. "I can't believe I have a police officer on speed dial." He parked at the curb.

"And, I can't believe this happened again." She pressed her hands to her face.

"Hey, come here." He helped her slide over next to him.

It was only a couple minutes before a police car came around the corner.

"Well, at least this time the lights aren't flashing and no siren. The neighbors are really going to be wondering about me. They'll be happy to see me go."

They got out to greet the officers, then waited while the men disappeared into the house. A tan sedan pulled up behind them and Hall got out.

"I didn't expect to see you so soon," he said as he approached.

"Didn't want to give you any time to sleep," Quinn said in return.

"I was hoping to sometime tonight. Do you want to tell me again what happened?"

"There's not much I can tell you. I was bringing Emily home. We found the window on the kitchen door broken out and called you."

"You didn't go in?" Hall asked.

"No, the door looked like it was ajar so we stayed out in case there was someone still inside, and we didn't want to mess up anything."

"Good thinking. Why don't you wait here and I'll go talk to the officers." Hall reached the house as the two men in police gear stepped out. They conferred for a few minutes before Hall returned.

"No one was in the house. Do you want to come check it out?" The detective led the way without waiting for them to answer.

Emily held on to Quinn's arm as they walked in. Cabinet doors stood open, but hadn't been emptied. The family room looked much the same. The trunk she used as a table was open, as was the coat closet, things thrown on the floor. Every door and cabinet in her house stood ajar. The dust ruffle on her bed was tossed up. The sight of her bed brought to fact that anywhere the sewing box could be had been searched, no smaller places disturbed.

Tears leaked from her eyes. She fought them back. It wasn't over.

"When did you say you were here last?" Detective Hall asked.

Emily opened her mouth to answer but could get nothing out.

"Last night. We swung by to get her some clothes. Left shortly six," Quinn answered.

"I take it wasn't like this?" Hall motioned to the room.

"No." Quinn fought to hold in his frustration.

The detective blew out a breath. “Then I’d say we still have a problem. I’d like to get a team over here, though I really don’t think we’ll find anything.”

“Do you need to have us hang around, or can I get Emily out of here?” Quinn fought to hold down his frustration.

The man looked thoughtful for a minute. “No, if you’ll give us permission and a key. I’ll see it’s locked up when we leave and find something to cover the window pane.”

“Thanks,” Quinn said. “Is it all right if she grabs some clothes?”

“Sure, just try not to touch any knobs or handles. I’ll swing by later to get your finger prints so we can eliminate them from any we find.”

“Thank you.” Emily finally found her voice.

“You’re welcome. Try not to worry. We’ll figure this out,” Hall assured before he turned to pull out his phone, taking several pictures of her room.

“Thank you,” Emily said again this time to Quinn.

“For what?”

“Being here.”

“You’re not going to argue about going back to my place?” He stood with his hands on her waist.

“No. All I want right now is to cuddle up with you and watch the sunset.”

“I think that can be arranged.” He leaned forward and placed a kiss on her forehead. “That is if you’ll do one thing for me.”

“What’s that?” She tipped her head slightly to the right.

“Pack a suitcase this time.”

A small laugh escaped her as she realized what he was saying. Every time they came over here something else happen. “I think I can do that?”

ଓଃ

For the first time, Emily was in Quinn's house all alone. Quinn had an important meeting he had to attend. It took all her persuasive talent to convince him he didn't need to reschedule and that she was safe. Finally, it was the promise she wouldn't leave the house, even to go into the backyard, for him to concede to go.

In all actuality, Emily figured the time was probably going faster for her than it was for him. Once more, she'd gotten lost in her exploration of the attic. She had quite a large pile of things for him to go through to just get rid of, some garbage, other stuff the girls could sell. He'd have to look over it first, but she was pretty sure which way it would go.

She also had a small section of things she was hoping he would let her purchase. With just a little TLC and a few changes, they could be lovely again. The door chime interrupted her pleasure.

A touch of anxiety hit out of nowhere, eliciting a shiver from deep within her. She stood, making it to the window on shaky knees. The car in the driveway was a new, sporty model with an outrageous sticker price.

She thought about running down stairs to answer the door, but her promise to Quinn came to mind. Satisfied with her non-action, she watched as a well-dressed man headed back down the walk to his car and drove away. She started to turn back to her project when the realization that she was hungry hit her.

In the kitchen, she pulled out leftovers from the fridge and slid them into the microwave. Her attention fell on the items still scattered on the table. When the bell chimed, she took out the plate and settled next to the sewing box.

As she ate, she picked up each piece of jewelry, inspecting them to make sure no genuine stones hid in the mix. As before, nothing stood out. She spread items into groups of what would have been in the original sewing box and what junk made its way in at a later time.

Keys, she fingered the one around her neck. There were thirteen others on the table. She arranged them in order of size.

The three smallest were the tiny type like those used for diaries or the old locks on suitcases that didn't do much. Four were the type for padlocks. Two newer house styles. She picked up one, rubbing at the tarnish on it. She set the keys to the side.

After eating, she'd take them around and try locks in the house. That left four older skeleton type, three much smaller and all plainer than the one she wore. Each she guessed was probably just as old. Once more, she touched the key on her necklace.

What do you go to? Does it even still exist?

She edged the keys to the side and focused on the letters. Last night after they returned home, she just hadn't had it in her to read them. Now, she hoped Quinn wouldn't mind her not waiting for him.

Taking her dishes to the sink, she washed her hands and returned to the table. Picking up the letters, she headed to the sunroom. Emily didn't know why that was where she picked to settle down, but like her relationship with Quinn, it was the right place to be.

Emily kicked her shoes off and curled up on the couch. Tucking one of the sky blue pillows under her arm, she picked up the first page, noticing her hand trembled slightly. Her heart thundered. She didn't know why but felt there was a key to her life inside. Taking a breath, she carefully unfolded the paper and read.

Today was the most unbelievable day of my life. I've never known such fear, even after my parents died. I also felt the greatest excitement and joy. I do not know what to call it, but I think I fell in love. I'll try to explain and maybe doing so I will be able to figure it out.

I just don't know where to begin. It involves two men who couldn't be more different. I admit I've noticed them both around.

The first, Ethan Lawson, I've never spoken to before today except a couple pleasantries on the street. Though, I will admit, I noticed him. I couldn't help but to. He is a fine looking man. Tall, one of the tallest men in town. He works construction, so he is strong. Slightly rugged looking, but he has the sweetest smile, and his eyes, I've never seen the likes. They are like a misty glade in fall, filled with blues, greens and gold.

Emily thought of Quinn. The letter could've been describing him.

So yes, I noticed him, but I never thought that he might have noticed me.

The other man, Oliver Armitstead, I'm afraid I have met on several occasions since coming to live with Aunt Lucille. He has approached me several times soliciting the opportunity to see me socially. Aunt Lucille said I should be flattered, but I cannot. Though he is the bank president, a respected, wealthy, powerful man here in town, for some reason that I haven't been able to explain until today, he has always left me with an uneasy feeling.

I think it was the way he watches me. It sends shivers up my spine. I admit it felt unwholesome to me, and I shunned him.

This evening, I was late leaving the shop because I had to finish some alterations. I left through the backdoor because I had seen him out front. I had just locked the door when I heard someone behind me. I turned to see Mr. Armitstead coming down the alley.

I nodded a greeting as I tried to step past, but he moved in front of me, cutting off the way. I felt a touch of fear but nothing compared to what his words to me conjured. He said he tried to be civil and patient but he was tired of waiting, and who did I think I was to defy him. I was just a little shop girl who should have been flattered by his attention. That he would have given me a fine life.

Then he grabbed me, pulling me toward him. That was when I knew true fear, for I knew what he intended to do. I screamed, but he struck me and clamped a hand over my mouth and shoved me against the wall. I fought with all my might, but I knew it wasn't enough. The world started to fade, for with his hand over my mouth, I could hardly breathe.

Suddenly I dropped to the ground, free. As my head cleared, I heard the brutal sounds of a fight. I raised my head to see Ethan Lawson grappling with him. As I watched, I feared for Ethan. Armitstead was not a fair fighter, but Ethan was the superior man. With a solid blow to Mr. Armitstead's jaw, Ethan laid him out unconscious, then he turned to me with such gentleness as I have never known from a man other than my father.

Ethan knelt beside me, wiped away my tears then slid his arms around me. In that instant I felt sheltered, safe, but more, I felt like I was where I was meant to be. I have been led to believe that is not how it is supposed to be. That if you're fortunate, love will grow as you toil together in life, but I know for me, it will not be so, for my heart belongs to one man. Ethan Lawson will hold it forever.

Aunt Lucille would probably try to convince me it was a case of hero worship if she knew the facts, but in all honesty it is not, for truth be told, I have had these feelings for him from the very first time I saw him. Just as I detested Mr. Armitstead, I have felt a connection to Ethan, even though I never spoke with him.

I guess writing this letter has truly laid it out plain in my mind.

I love Ethan Lawson.

Emily brushed at the tears on her cheek. Carefully, laying the page down, Emily wrapped her arms around her body, staring off at nothing. Sarah had fallen in love with Ethan on sight. She knew it after one meeting.

She couldn't help but compare it to how she felt for Sarah's great-grandson. From the moment she saw Quinn, she felt a pull on her heart, and now after only a couple days, he seemed to have taken up residence there.

She had tried using logic and what she thought of as compatibility in choosing a husband, thinking that love would grow. Obviously, it hadn't been that way for her. For like Ethan had been for Sarah, Quinn Lawson was the man for her. Emily let the truth beat unrestrained in her heart awhile longer before picking up the next letter.

The next several were from friends Sarah had left behind on moving in with her aunt. There was a letter that contained a photograph of a man in uniform. Emily figured the letter was to Sarah's mother from a brother who was in the First World War. There were also three postcards from the same man, but that was all.

She found a letter from Aunt Lucille with condolences on the loss of her parents and urging Sarah to come live with her. Reading the letter, Emily got that Aunt Lucille was a kind-hearted woman, but also a no-nonsense one. It seemed she never had children of her own, and welcomed Sarah in. Emily decided she wanted to find out more about the woman.

The letter Emily saved for last was to Sarah from Ethan. It was written in bold, precise script. Once more, her breath caught as she started to read.

My dearest Sarah,

I am not a man of poetry or fancy words, but at this moment I wish it were so. Tomorrow I will take you as my wife. I count the minutes. I am a most fortunate man, for I knew the moment I first saw you, you were the one for me.

You do not know how hard it was just to say hello to you. You took my breath each time you smiled at me. I do not know how long it would've taken me to approach you. I fear if fate hadn't stepped in, it might have been too late. I count it a blessing that fate did place me passing the alley at the exact time you needed me, though I will admit, I walked that way daily in hopes to catch just a glimpse of you.

I wanted to ask you to marry me that very day, for I knew when you looked up at me, with tears in your beautiful blue eyes, I loved you. I feared because what had been a dreadful moment for you might cause you to shirk from me, but my world became right when you tucked yourself against my heart.

Now I worry our country is in for a trying time, but I promise I will take good care of you forever. You need not have concerns of my being able to provide for you. Besides my grubstake, and because of the dreadful incidence, I have rid myself of all my investments and took all my money from the bank at a most opportune time.

I know it is not done for a man to talk about such matters with his intended or many would say even his wife, but I want us always to be one in everything we face. I want you to know that, though my wealth is secured in gold and money, you are my greatest treasure. For even if I would have ended up a poor man, with you at my side, I still would have been rich. You are my greatest love. I look forward to our days together, for you hold my heart forever.

Yours, Ethan.

Emily dropped the letter in her lap, and brought her hands to her chin as she fought to snivel in her tears. "Ohh." She let out at the love she'd just read.

"Emily." Quinn crossed to her as she raised her tear-streaked face to him. He dropped down beside her, one hand going to her face, his other arm sliding around her. "What is it, sweetheart?"

The endearment brought more tears and a little laugh. “I’m okay. It’s just so beautiful.”

“What?” Confusion swept away his alarm.

“The letters. I hope you don’t mind. I read them. Your great-grand parents loved each other so much. It is just so sweet.” She leaned forward and kissed him, then settled against him, rubbing her cheek against his chest. “How was your day?”

“Good, but a whole lot better now.” He shifted next to her, toed off his shoes and placed his feet on the ottoman, tucking her closer into him. “This is a nice welcome home. I could get to liking it. Minus the tears.”

She gave him a squeeze.

“So are you going to tell me about the letters?”

Emily reached back with one hand to lift the stack off the end table. “This letter and these cards.” She showed one postcard of New York City and two with soldiers on them to him. “I think were from Sarah’s Uncle to her mother. These are from friends, and this is Aunt Lucille instructing her to come after her parent’s deaths.”

“This one, was Sarah to herself. It talks about the story you told the girls about the banker attacking her because she shunned his advances. Your great-grandfather came to her rescue. It’s all true. Sarah was writing out her thoughts. She already had a crush on Ethan, though they’d only exchanged a few words. When he rescued her, she knew she loved him.”

Emily raised her gaze to him. “Did you know, you have your great-grandfather’s eyes? When Sarah described them, it was like she was describing yours.”

“Really?”

“Yes, Sarah loved his eyes.”

“And what do you think of mine?” His voice grew husky.

“I love them.” Her heart pounded as she said the words.

"I love your eyes, too. Such a beautiful blue." He brushed a strand of hair, then caught it in his fingers to play with it.

"Oh, Sarah had blue eyes." She lifted the letter she dropped in her lap just before he came in. "This is from Ethan to Sarah the night before they got married. He says he's not poetic but I think it's beautiful. You can feel his love for her."

Quinn took the letter from her and started to read aloud.

Emily brushed back tears again as he ended.

"I can understand how he felt." He set the letter on the end table and placed the others with it. He shifted so they ended up facing each other. "It was a simpler time back then, when a couple decided to marry, quite often it was done without much delay. Not like today where couples move in together for years first. When hard times came, they didn't just give up and move on, they worked together. Maybe we need more old fashion love in the world."

"You're a touch poetic, too." She studied his face.

Quinn erupted in laughter. "I don't have a poetic bone in my body."

Emily wanted to argue with him on that, but didn't get the chance to because his cell phone rang. It ended up being Payton. The siblings chatted for a minute while Emily relaxed against him, then Quinn said, "Yes, I've seen her again." He looked down and grinned. "In fact, she's right here. Would you like to say hi?" He held out his phone. "Payton likes you."

Emily took the offered phone, not sure what to say. "Hello."

"My brother does have sense, who knew." Payton's words were so unexpected Emily burst into laughter. "I was just checking up on him and wondered if you two would like to join Richard and me for dinner tonight. The girls were invited to a friends to watch a movie that just released, and since we're free, we decided to go out to dinner. I was going to try a little match making, but guess I didn't need to."

"Would you like to go to dinner with your sister and her husband?" Emily tipped the phone away and asked Quinn.

"Sure, if that's okay with you."

"Sounds good." Turning back to the phone. "Where do we meet you and when?" Emily repeated the time and place to Quinn, who nodded.

"Okay," she said back in the phone.

"I'm not interrupting am I?" Payton asked. "You didn't have other plans?"

"No. We were just reading some letters of your great-grandmother's we found in the sewing box I bought."

"Really?" Payton sounded interested. "I'd love to see them."

"We'll bring them so you can take and read them." She looked to Quinn for his approval.

He nodded.

"You'll love them. They are so precious. We'll see you in a little bit." She disconnected and handed the phone back to Quinn. "That is okay, isn't it?"

"Yes. And technically those are yours, you bought them."

"No," Emily said firmly. "No matter what happens, those are yours. Your family should have them. They're special."

"So are you." He kissed the end of her nose.

"What I am is dirty." She looked at the jeans she wore. "I need to grab a quick shower before we go. I'll be fast." She sprang up, running for her room leaving Quinn to gather the letters.

True to her word, Emily was back down stairs twenty-five minutes later, and they made it to the Thai restaurant at the same time Payton and her husband pulled in.

They each ordered a different dish to share around the table.

"This is wonderful." Emily sighed as the food was sat before them.

They ate and talked. Emily told them about herself while she learned about Payton and Richard.

"I really lucked out with Richard," Payton said. "I met Richard in college and he hadn't realized who my family was until we'd gone on quite a few dates, and we'd already clicked. He'd just thought I was the pretty girl that was interested in architecture along with interior design."

"No," Richard interrupted. "I thought you were a beautiful woman, who was interested in architecture and not there just because the class was mostly guys."

"Oh, you did that very nicely." Payton leaned over and kissed him.

"Thank you." Richard accepted and returned the kiss. "Actually, I saw her the first day, and as my grandmother would say, she knocked my socks off. I knew I had to move fast before one of the other guys got to her. I didn't believe it when one of the guys told me who she really was."

"What he's not saying is that the guy was trying to break us up. He tried to convince Richard I was just using him. It was revenge because he'd asked me out and I refused. I'd seen the way he acted and wasn't interested at all. Besides, I kind of fell for Richard when I first saw him in the hall. It didn't take me long to know he was the one I wanted."

Emily glanced at Quinn. Her breath caught. She knew what it felt like to have her socks knocked off.

The conversation continued with antics of the girls until Payton glanced at the time. "We'd better go pick up the girls. What a great evening."

"It's been nice being out," Emily agreed.

"I still can't believe what you've been going through. I'm so glad Quinn has been there for you."

Emily glanced at Quinn who was talking with Richard about designs for the new sub-division. The two men had resisted all through dinner, but Quinn wanted to pass on a few points that had been covered in his meeting that day. When she looked back, she found Payton smiling at her. "Did I miss something?"

Payton's smile broadened. "You're in love with my brother."

The instinct to deny it flicked across Emily's mind then disappeared as pleasure flowed through her. "Yeah." She couldn't hold it in, her attention going back to Quinn.

"If it helps, I was watching him through dinner, and trust me, I've never seen him like he is with you. I don't know if he's told you he was engaged before."

"He did."

"She was beautiful, but wasn't good for him. Didn't make him happy. She didn't even care. Sorry, I can't say I liked her." Payton winced. "The thing is, I like you, but more important, Quinn does too. He's been looking for a long time. I better stop talking now before I mess things up."

"It's okay." Emily reached for her hand. "I know what you're saying. We're trying to take things slow. The feelings have come so fast, but Quinn knows I love him."

"And she knows I love her." Quinn slipped back in the conversation, sliding his arm around Emily.

"Wow." Payton exclaimed. "I've never heard you say that before."

"I never have. But, don't say a word to Mom and Dad," Quinn asked.

"I promise," Payton assured.

"Come on." Richard helped Payton up then draped his arm around his wife. "Let's go home before you start to meddle. Give them time my little matchmaker."

"I concede," Payton said as they walked out. "Bye. Thanks for the copies of the letters." Payton gave Emily then Quinn a hug before her husband steered her to their car.

Quinn wrapped his arm around Emily in a way that was becoming natural. "Are you feeling overwhelmed yet?"

"No. I like your sister and Richard. I think it was a great evening."

"Good. I enjoy being around my family. We like to get together," he said as he opened the car door for her.

"I wish I could say that." A wistful quality tinted her voice.

"Do you want children?" Quinn asked cautiously a minute later as they pulled out of the driveway. He knew a lot of women didn't. Now he looked back, Charlotte said she did but he doubted it.

"Yes, I'm kind of hoping between three and five."

"Was Greg okay with that?" For some reason, he couldn't see the man with a lot of kids.

Emily laughed. "No, you pegged that right," she answered as if she knew his thoughts. "He wanted to be the main focus. Kids would have taken away from him. His plan was to wait several years, minimum of five, then have a baby. If it was a boy, be done. If a girl, we'd wait a couple more years and try for a boy again. If that was another girl, we'd be done."

Quinn glanced over at her then back to the road. "You were okay with that?"

"No. It had me wondering. One of the reasons I wouldn't commit to a wedding date, which was fine with him."

"He thought he could talk you into sleeping with him." Quinn realized.

"I think so, but it wasn't happening. I was so foolish."

"I don't think so. I think inside you knew and just let yourself be talked into … going along because he needed it. You are a very serving person. He saw it and used it."

Quinn was silent a minute. "Emily you aren't … with me … only trying to help me?"

"No!" she came back immediately then dropped her voice. "You're not with me just to help me?"

"Definitely not. I … I can't seem to think of my life without you now. That sounds so … we've only know each other a week, and I don't want to be without you. So much for not rushing things," he said derisively.

She laughed. "We are quite the pair aren't we? We both should be gun shy about relationships, and what are we doing, falling right into one."

He grinned. "Yeah, but I'm not going to complain, because this one does feel right. I'm thinking, maybe like my great-grandfather, fate is taking a hand. And, just so you know, I'm good with girls."

"After seeing you with your nieces, I can guess that."

"Yeah, they're pretty fun."

"I've set some things off to the side for them, if they're going to have another sale." She watched his hand on the steering wheel. He had good looking hands.

"If you tell them that, they will."

His words pulled her attention went back to the girls. "You'll have to approve anything I put there."

"I'm sure it's fine. Much better than I did before. For the life of me, and I've thought hard about it, I really don't remember putting the sewing box in the pile. Payton asked the girls about it, and they didn't put it there either."

Emily reached over and placed her hand over his on the gearshift. "You get to have the box back."

"No." He turned his hand over, linking their fingers. "That wasn't what I was getting at."

"I know." She gave his hand a squeeze.

"I'm thinking it kind of goes back to the fate thing. Maybe I do believe in it. What are the odds, it ended up there, and you bought it." He turned the car into the driveway.

“Quinn!” Emily’s hand came up to point at the breezeway.

“What?” He released her hand to grip the wheel.

“A man.” Her fingers trembled as they came up to point at a fleeing figure.

Chapter Thirteen

Quinn's gaze followed the direction Emily pointed. The man had already disappeared around the corner of the garage, but he didn't doubt her. "Stay here." He shoved the car into park. "And lock the doors." He was out and running before she even had a chance to protest.

Quinn rounded the corner, lights lit the yard, but he didn't see anyone. Coming to a stop, he listened. There were no chorus of crickets, cicadas or other night bugs. It was totally quiet. A rustling in the trees, drew his attention and he took off after it.

Fifty feet in, he froze and waited again. Nothing. His thoughts went to Emily alone in the car. If there was trouble surely she'd blast the horn. He turned, scanning all directions. In the distance, he heard a dog bark, a second later a car started up. Quinn blew out a breath. Knowing it was futile, he headed back.

The moment he stepped into the breezeway, Emily was out of the car and running to him. She grabbed him. "Don't you ever do that to me again!" Tightening her hands in his shirt. "What if he had a gun?"

Quinn wrapped his arms around her and pulled her into his arms. The hug wasn't near long enough but he wanted to get them inside. Releasing her, he led her to the door, unlocked it and fairly pushed her into the mudroom. "I'll be right back." He ran back to his car and pulled it into the garage.

Locking the door behind him, he jogged through the breezeway. Emily opened the door before he reached it. The moment he entered the security code, she was back in his arms. Her hold was fierce and she trembled. "You scared me to death."

Quinn didn't answer because he knew he couldn't give her the answer she wanted without lying. If the incidence ever arose again, he'd do the same but hopefully catch them. "It's okay. I'm all right," He murmured against her temple, followed by the brush of his lips. "Come on. Let's go into the other room." He led her into his den, settling down beside her before pulling out his phone.

He rang Detective Hall, expecting to get his voicemail. The man answered on the second ring.

"Hall."

"Sorry to disturb you detective. I was just going to leave you a message. This is Quinn Lawson. We had a prowler tonight, but he got away before I could get a look at him."

"You went after him. Of course you did." His recognition came through the phone. "You certain he's gone?"

"Yeah," Quinn said dejectedly. "I heard a car. I'm pretty positive it was him."

"You're safe now?"

"Yes."

"He didn't get into the house?" Hall asked.

"No. The alarm was set and hadn't been tripped."

"Okay. I'll get a car to patrol the neighborhood, just in case. Can you give me a description?"

Quinn looked down at Emily. "Can you describe him?" Quinn activated the speaker.

"Not really. Just it was a man. He wore dark pants and a dark jacket. He was back lit." She thought a second.

Quinn could see her going over the image in her mind.

After a second, she started again. "The jacket was a windbreaker type. The lighter weight kind of puffy at the sleeves and body, so hard to tell his shape."

She breathed out and in very slow and steady. "He was about two feet taller than the rose bush there. About six feet. He wore a cap. Again, he was back lit, so all dark outline." Her voice faded out. "The light glinted off the emblem on it, but the emblem was black or at least dark like the cap." She sighed. "That's it. I only saw him for a couple seconds."

"That was good. I'll pass it on. I'll be out first thing in the morning when we have some light. I will ask you to have the sprinklers not run."

"They already ran. I kicked them on earlier this evening when we'd left to go out to dinner because it's been dry the last couple days. I don't have it set on auto yet."

"That's real good. I'll see you in the morning. Please don't go out into the yard until I get there." With that Hall hung up

"I think he's beginning to wonder about us," Emily said with mirth in her voice.

"And I thought we were such a normal couple." He stroked a hand over her hair. "So what would you like to do?"

"Something light to break the stress."

"I have an animated movie that just released that I bought for the girls. I haven't watched it yet."

"That sounds wonderful." She smiled, thinking of him watching it with his nieces. He was a good man. He would be a good father. And, he wouldn't mind having daughters.

Quinn finished opening the package, slid the movie in to the play and came back to settle next to her. By the second song, she relaxed and settled into the rightness in his arms.

ଔଷ

He watched them through the large window. It had been risky coming back, especially since he couldn't get in. He'd seen the police car drive by. Luckily, he'd moved his car over another street, into the driveway of an elderly woman he worked for and knew to be out of town.

Frustration burned in him. If Wallace had just done what he was supposed to, none of this would be happening. He'd have the key, the map and the gold by now and no one would have been the wiser about its existence.

Now Lawson and the woman were looking into things. As were the police. He needed to get that box before they found the map. It had to still be in the box. He wouldn't accept any other possibility.

The question was, was there any reference to the hidden gold in the house that Lawson might stumble on when going through papers? When he'd talked to him, the man didn't seem to know anything about it, nor had his grandfather on a visit before the old man died. He thought that so peculiar. He had to know of his father's distaste for banks, that after the crash he never trusted all his wealth to banks, keeping his original 'grubstake' hidden away. Just in case.

The thought burned in his mind like acid. The land and money the family had accumulated all those years ago should have been his grandfather's. Should have been his.

He watched a little longer. He'd get that key, the map, then find the treasure. No one would be the wiser. He'd get even. It was history all over again. Because of a woman, things were ruined.

A century ago, all had been lost because of the little shop girl that the elder Lawson had rescued and married. How could someone so insignificant cause such chaos? He stared at the woman he could see snuggled into Quinn Lawson's side. She was just as much trouble. Maybe as his grandfather failed to do, he should get rid of her. The thought settled in his mind. Maybe he should get rid of both her and Lawson.

Satisfied, he turned away. It was time to make new plans.

Chapter Fourteen

"Careful. Don't hurt yourself," Quinn said as they carried the old dresser along the breezeway to the garage. "How did I ever let you talk me into moving this stuff this morning? We should've waited until the weekend for Richard to come help me."

"I needed it out of the way, and once again, I'm fine. This isn't that heavy, just bulky, and we brought it downstairs in the elevator, which would have been the hard part," Emily pointed out. "Besides, who do you think moved all my stuff when I moved here?"

"I would hope you had help."

"I did when I moved out, but I didn't know anyone in town when I got here, so I unloaded most on my own. I'm tough." She grinned over the dresser at him. "Watch your step."

"So after we get the rest of it moved out of here, have you figured out your plans for the rest of the day?"

"I was thinking while you make your calls, I'd take all the keys around and see if I can find what they go to. With this out of the attic, it will give me a little more room to work. You know, there is some really amazing things up there, and I'm hardly even a tenth of the way through."

"I have to admit, I'm kind of glad it's you doing it and not me."

"You owe me," Emily said as they moved through the open bay door.

"Big time. What would you like? A trip to Rome, Paris, a cruise? You name it."

She laughed. "I'll think about it."

"You know, my calls shouldn't take much more than an hour. Why don't you get started inside with your treasure hunt and I'll come help you."

They set the dresser down and he came to drape his arm around her shoulders. "You really are pretty tough. Hey, I have something to show you before we go in."

Quinn led her up the stairs on the side of the garage. He opened the door and stepped back to let her enter before him.

"Wow, this is nice, I didn't realize there was an apartment up here. Though I should have from the outside." She looked around the open-concept room filled with sunlight coming from side windows and two sky lights. Sitting in one corner was a small kitchen with white cabinets and an island that separated it from the large living space. The whole floor was covered in a grayish wood looking tile which added to the airy feel of the room.

"It only has one bedroom, but it takes up the whole area back here." Quinn motioned to an open door that led to the room filled with warm sunlight from another skylight besides the window. "The bathroom is here and there is a small storage room there. He opened another door opposite to the bathroom entrance."

"This really is a great use of space. Nicely done."

"It originally was to be the gardener's apartment, but wasn't occupied as that for about thirty years. We remodeled it for me during college. I was working on projects in the area during the summer. It let me have freedom, and I was still close to the house if grandpa needed me. It's hooked to the intercom system in the house." He motioned to the panel on the wall.

"This is great. I love all the natural light."

"I was thinking." He walked over to her, reaching out to take her hand, rubbing his thumb over her knuckles. "You have to be out of your place in about six weeks, and I know with everything going on you haven't had time to look for something new. If you don't find anything, you could move in here."

"Quinn."

"Rent would be cheap. I know the owner. And, with all the light, it would make a great studio to work in. Besides, it would give you access to the sunroom," he added with a grin.

"And," she drew the word out. "What if things don't work out between us?" Emily managed to get the words out past her pounding heart.

"We'll face that if it happens, but for some reason I'm not worried about it, and I hope if it does, we'll remain friends. I enjoy being with you."

"I enjoy being with you, too." Tears threatened with the emotion coursing through her. "I'll think about it."

"Good." He kissed her, a light breezy contact. "Let's get the rest of the junk moved."

"Not junk, treasures," she countered following him outside.

"Some of its junk."

"Okay, I'll give you that, but we have today's junk all out. You know," she said as he reached the bottom step. "It's unfair adding the sunroom to the offer."

He turned and laughed at her. "I'm learning your weaknesses and hedging my bets."

Standing on the step, they were at eye level. Emily got lost in the amazing combination of blues, greens and golds. "Sarah was right. Such beautiful eyes. I could look into them forever."

He eased closer with her words. "Forever sounds good." It was as if his lips brushed hers with each syllable, before settling there. His phone rang cutting off the kiss way too soon.

"Quinn." His father's voice greeted him when he connected. "You sound a little breathless. Did I interrupt something?"

"Just carrying some stuff from the attic to the garage." He grinned at Emily and mouthed "my father". He wondered if his parents had been talking with Payton.

Emily nodded and motioned to the attic indicating she was going up.

Quinn caught her hand and moved with her while his father talked in his ear.

"That's quite a project. I can help you some when your mother and I get there. You still planning on us?"

"I am, and there's someone I want you to meet." He twitched his eyebrows at Emily, when she looked up at him in shock. "She even agreed to come over one morning and make you crepes."

"You're setting yourself up," she whispered.

He tipped the phone away from his mouth and covered the speaker. "They need to know. Besides, I bet Payton's already blabbed." He turned his attention back to the phone as they entered the house.

"I'm interested in meeting her," his father said pretty much confirming his suspicion about Payton. "But why I called is, I wanted to go over a few things with you before our phone conference this morning."

With a squeeze to Emily's hand, Quinn broke off and headed for his den.

Emily went through the kitchen to the breakfast nook where the sewing box and contents were still laid out on the table. One by one, she picked up each key and tried to decide what they'd go to.

The smaller ones she put in one of her pants pockets, the larger in the other pocket and headed up stairs. In the attic, she started going down the rows looking for anything with a key. For the amount of stuff up there, it was amazingly organized, so she could see most things.

Within an hour, she found two padlocks that fit two of the keys. A bike lock that fit another, a sideboard and hutch that fit one of the skeleton type, a briefcase that matched, and another to an old makeup case similar to one she remembered her grandmother having.

"How you coming?" Quinn said coming up the stairs.

"Actually, good. I've located about where half the keys go."

"I'm impressed."

"I've been fortunate. These were easy to reach. There's a trunk I can see back here that I'm trying to get to."

He came over to help her slide several boxes and chairs out of the way to reveal the vintage, dome-top steamer trunk.

"Are you all done?" She gave one last push on a box and dug the remaining keys out of one pocket.

"Not quite. I have a conference call that starts in about twenty minutes. I just came to check on you and add some muscle for a minute."

"Perfect timing. This is beautiful, isn't it?" She ran a hand over the top of the trunk.

"You know, a week ago I probably would have just called it an old trunk, but yeah I can see what you mean. It looks like it should hold buried treasure." He rattled the lock.

"Let's see if any of these three fit. I'm afraid this one might be too long," she said as she slid the first one in. It didn't work." She studied the other two and picked one. "Cross your fingers." Her breath caught as she stuck it in the lock and turned. It shifted then caught. Emily applied a little more pressure and with a faint grind the lock popped open. "It worked." She looked up, bursting with excitement.

Quinn smiled back just as big. "You're pretty good at this treasure hunting thing."

She couldn't stop smiling. "I didn't tell you how many things I tried, that the keys didn't work in."

"So you're saying I have a lot more keys around here somewhere."

"I'm afraid so, but fortunately all but one suitcase was already unlocked. And it didn't sound like anything was in it."

"The old shake it method?"

"You got it. Do you want to do the honors?" She motioned to the trunk.

He removed the padlock.

Emily took it, laying it carefully on the floor as he lifted the lid. She held her breath once more, anxious to see what might be hidden within. She hadn't found anything of great importance today, but there was always hope.

The breath whooshed out of her at the first sight of the pile of papers with a few old pictures scattered within. She looked at Quinn to gauge his reaction. He looked slightly in awe as he reached out and lifted a picture lying on top. The date on the corner read August 1939. A man and a woman with two small boys, the youngest only three or four years old, stood by a car with a long nose and large fenders over white-walled tires. Even in the black and white photo you could see the car was shiny new.

"Sarah and Ethan?" Emily asked pointing to the couple.

Quinn nodded, clearing his throat. "This would have been Owen." He pointed to the older boy. "And my grandfather, James. Thank you." He leaned over and kissed her cheek.

"You would've found it anyway," she pointed out.

"Eventually, maybe. Come on, let's take this trunk down to the den. Later this evening we can explore it in comfort."

Together they carried it to the elevator. I'll see you in a little while," Quinn said as the door closed.

It was almost an hour before Emily gave up. Stretching up so high that her fingertips brushed the ceiling, she decided on taking a break from the attic. For all the success in finding what the keys belonged to in the first hour, she had absolutely none in the second. A little discouraged she headed down the stairs, deciding to look around the main floor for possibilities and a different view. She could hear Quinn talking in the den, obviously still on his conference call, she didn't linger to listen.

Starting first in the living room, she wandered around looking for anything that required a key. She didn't find anything so moved into the dining room only to come up empty again. The grandfather clock in the entry had a place for a key, but she found the key inside. She blew out a breath.

"Ready for a break," Quinn asked, stepping out of the den.

"Yes, my investigative aptitude seems to have fizzled out."

"Let's grab some lunch and look at what we still have." He caught her hand and drew her across the hall into the kitchen.

They worked together making an Asian chicken salad then sat down at the table to eat.

Emily pulled the remaining keys from her pockets, placing them on the table. "So six left."

"That's amazing. Going with the odds, I can't believe you located that many. You can't feel bad about that."

"I guess not, and I'm not done looking yet. I just needed a change of scenery, and I was hoping to find something to figure out what the man was after."

"I can't help with what he was after, but how about we go for a walk after lunch?" he suggested.

"That sounds wonderful. We can go clean around the bench."

"I was thinking something more like a plain walk, something totally different. Like maybe old town, down by the river. We can wander the shops, swing in for pastries. Maybe grab dinner there before we come home."

"That sounds wonderful. You are talking about several hours." She arched an eyebrow at him.

"I feel guilty that I'm working you too much. That was not my plan on bringing you here." His hand brushed hers, then settled on it.

"Really. You had a plan?"

"I did." He lowered his voice. "A totally nefarious one."

"Really? Is it a secret?"

He leaned closer and whispered. "I wanted you to like it so much here, you'd never want to leave. How am I doing?"

"Not bad," she answered back, then paused before continuing. "But I'm afraid it's not your house that's winning me over." Butterflies flittered in her chest then erupted into a flurry when his gaze met hers.

"That is really good to know. So do we have a date?"

"I'll go change. Can you give me forty minutes?"

"I'll give you whatever time you want."

Emily felt like there was a double meaning to his words, and a promise more than a simple date behind the second. "I'll be back down here in forty minutes." The words were drawn out and breathy but she couldn't help it. She stared at him a full minute before finally being able to drag her gaze away and dash for the stairs.

ઉઢ્ઢ

Exactly forty minutes later Emily came running down the stairs. Her hair hung in glorious waves down her back. Her lips glistened a dewy, soft pink that Quinn wanted to taste. Not that he didn't always want to every time he looked at them. Emily called to him like no woman ever had. She was his personal siren, but he had no fear of her leading him to doom.

Nothing had ever felt so right as they walked the shops of old town together. This is what he'd been missing in all other relationships he'd ever had. The natural link and comfort. What he felt with Emily was what he'd always dreamed of. What he saw in his parent's relationship. The just right vibe.

In one shop window, Quinn saw some charming old household items that had been decorated into making them beautiful accent pieces. "Those are nice. They remind me of you." He pointed them out.

"Thank you." Her eyes sparkled as she grinned.

"Wait a minute." He looked over at her. "You made those?"

"I did. This is the shop here in town that carries my pieces."

"I thought you sold on the internet."

"I do. But I have a couple shops that carry my stuff. Here and a couple of the resort towns that have a large tourist flow. They seem to draw a fair amount of attention. I don't make quite as much on the pieces because of the commission, but it's close because the shops tack part of that on the sale price."

"A savvy business woman. Come on let's go in." He tugged her hand, drawing her through the open door.

Together they wandered, as he tried to pick out which pieces were hers.

"You like them?" Emily asked, her voice sounding as if she was looking for his approval.

"I do. Some are just amazing. Who would've thought? Well obviously you did. You have quite a talent."

"Thank you."

He wrapped his arm around her as they exited a shop.

"What –"

Emily's question was cut off as he pulled her back, barely keeping her from running into someone.

"Oh," Emily gasped. "Excuse me."

"No problem." The man pulled back, then said, "Quinn, fancy meeting you here."

Quinn looked at him, finally recognizing the man he'd never seen out of one of his fancy suits before. "Oh, Oliver. Sorry. Didn't see you."

"With this lovely lady, I'm not surprised. I wouldn't be able to take my eyes off her either." His attention settled on Emily and didn't seem to shift, but she did. Quinn felt her turn into him slightly.

Quinn tightened his hold, feeling a protective surge. "Sorry. We'll get out of your way." He started to move her to the side, but before he could, the man stuck out his hand.

"Oliver Raine, I'm an estate lawyer for Quinn."

Tentatively, Emily reached out and shook the offered hand. "Emily London." She pulled her hand free, and brought it up to rest on Quinn's side.

"Emily, it's a pleasure to meet you."

"I didn't know you were dating anyone." Raine turned his attention to him. "Though, I can see why you'd want to keep her all to yourself."

Quinn knew it was meant to be a compliment, but like the trembling he could feel in Emily's fingers attested to, the words made him uneasy."

"We haven't been dating long. Sorry, we really need to go." Quinn started to steer her clear but Raine stopped them.

"Maybe you could help me a moment." He focused on Emily. "I like your necklace. I'm looking for a gift for my sister. Something like that would be perfect. Can I asked where you got it?"

Emily's hand came up to wrap around the key. "I made it. All my pieces are one of a kind, but this store has several pieces of jewelry and other items I made. If you ask them, they'll be happy to point them out."

"I'll do that." The lawyer's gaze flickered to the necklace locked in her hand and up so fast, that if Quinn wouldn't have been watching, he would have missed the action.

Raine's smile broadened, but held no true warmth. "Well, I'll just go inside and see what I can find. Have a nice evening."

"You, too." Quinn forced the words out.

"Pleasure to meet you, Miss London."

Emily nodded before Quinn steered her down the sidewalk. An itch between Quinn's shoulder blades suggested that if he looked back the man's gaze would be on them.

They'd gone about a hundred feet when air whooshed from Emily.

"Are you all right?" He stopped and turned her into his arms.

She nodded and took in a deep breath, letting it out slowly. "Yes, sorry. For some reason, your lawyer gives me the willies."

"He's not my lawyer," Quinn said firmly.

"But, he said."

"Technically, he works for the firm that handled my grandfather's estate. He oversaw all the paperwork for my grandfather's lawyer who had retired. Trust me, he never has, nor ever will be my lawyer. I can't say I like him any better than you do."

"And I can't say I don't like him. I don't know him. There's just something." She shrugged. "The willies."

"That's as good a way as any to sum it up. Though, for me, I felt like there was something going on under the surface." Quinn leaned forward and brushed his lips to her forehead. "Come on, let's continue our walk and find a place to eat. There's a nice little restaurant on the next block."

"Okay," Emily said.

Quinn didn't miss the quick glance over her shoulder as she fell into step with him, or the way she pressed into his side. He was more than happy to tighten his hold. She fit perfectly against him, and they moved easily together.

They reached the restaurant. He put their name on the waiting list, and they went to stand at the railing by the river. The sun started to sink in the sky setting off a glow of red and orange to the water as it rippled past.

"This is so beautiful." Emily leaned into Quinn as he slid his arm around her waist. "I came down to this area my first night in town before I found the cottage. It was here I knew I'd found the place for me. That kind of coming home feeling."

"I think mine was always the house. I couldn't wait for summers when I came to stay with my grandparents. Even though a lot of the house is formal, it was … my place."

She looked over at him. "I can understand that. I've seen you there, the heritage, and now you're making it your own."

"That's the plan."

"Lawson, party of two," the hostess called out.

"That's us."

They started to follow the woman when an alarm sound went off coming from Quinn's pocket.

"What's that?" Emily asked when he stopped abruptly, pulling out his phone.

"The house alarm. Someone's trying to break in. We have to go."

Chapter Fifteen

Red and blue lights flashed over the front of the old mansion when they turned the corner. Quinn was forced to pull to the side and stop before making it to the garage. Emily was out of the car before he could come around to get her. He caught her hand. They ran up the driveway only to be stopped by an officer before they could reach the door.

"I'm Quinn Lawson," Quinn said reaching for his wallet. "This is my house."

The officer waved them on after checking his license.

Since all the action seemed to be focused on the side of the house, they headed that way. Another officer started to stop them when Quinn's name was called from the breezeway.

"Heard the address and headed over," Detective Hall greeted them. "I think I should just set an office up here."

Quinn shook the hand extended to him. "Let me know if you need me to find you a space. Did whoever it was get in?"

"That's the question."

Quinn shifted to see around the detective. The door stood cracked open. The wood around the lock splintered.

Hall followed his gaze and led the way to it. "Unlike Miss London's house, whoever attempted this had no breaking and entering skills at all. Sammy was a pro, though it would have been doubtful if he could have handled your alarm. This guy didn't even try the lock. He went with the crowbar method. Either he didn't know about the alarm system or hoped you hadn't set it. Which, if that was the case, he's getting desperate. You haven't thought of anything he could be after?" The detective looked back and forth between them.

"No," Emily answered first.

"No," Quinn echoed.

"What about the key?" Hall pointed to her necklace. "Found what it goes to yet?"

"No," Emily said with a shake of her head.

"We found thirteen other keys in the box." Quinn took over. "Emily's placed seven of them so far. That leaves us with six."

"One is a tiny key. I really don't think we have to worry about that one," she added.

"Let's go in so you can have a look around." Hall led the way. "We don't think the intruder had much time. With all the activity you've been giving us, we've had a car in the area when possible. They got here in only a matter of a couple minutes."

"Nice response time," Quinn said.

"We try. It's presumed whoever it was fled when they heard the sirens."

"No!" The cry ripped from Emily, and she broke free to rush across the kitchen to the table. "It's gone. The sewing box."

"It's all right, Emily." Quinn came forward to take her arm, turning her to him. "I moved it while you were changing. I saw it and thought of what happened at your house. It being saved because it was under your bed. I moved it into the den with the trunk."

She visibly relaxed.

"You're right though," Quinn continued. "We better check on it."

They made their way to the den where they found the box sitting safely behind his desk. While Detective Hall went to release the other officers, Quinn and Emily went through the house to see if anything looked disturbed. Emily met the detective back in the den where they waited for Quinn.

"Everything looks fine. I think you're right," Quinn acknowledged. "The officers arrived before he had a chance to search for whatever he was after. Do you think it was the sewing box?"

"It tends to be a recurring element." The detective nodded to the box. "Have you found anything else?"

"Just several letters written by my great-grandparents, hidden under the bottom lining," Quinn said.

"Have you checked all the linings?"

Quinn looked to Emily.

"Not really." She picked up the box and set it on Quinn's desk, once more taking out everything in it. Together they lifted out the bottom panel and studied each seam. Everything else was tacked down.

"Nothing." Hill sat back, pursing his lips. "And you said there was nothing in the letters?"

"I don't think so," Quinn said. "Several were from friends and family, a couple postcards from war time."

"The two coolest was a letter – slash journal note of Quinn's great-grandparent's first meeting," Emily said. "His great-grandmother was attacked and he came to her rescue."

"Yeah, if it happened today it might have been a police matter, but all parties are long dead," Quinn continued. "So I can't see it being anything."

"The other cool letter was his great-grandfather to her the night before they were married. It was so sweet."

"But it pretty much just verified the history I knew about where the family wealth came from." When the detective looked interested, he continued. "After the attack,

Ethan, my great-grandfather, pulled all his money out of the bank and cashed out his investments. They were handled by the man who attacked my great-grandmother. That was a month before the stock market crash in 1929 when the market was at its highest point."

"Really." The detective looked intrigued.

"Yeah," Quinn said. "It left him a very wealthy man going into the depression. He already owned a lot of property and bought up a lot more during the time."

"So what happened to all that money, if he took it out of the bank? Did he move it to another bank?" Intrigue built in the detective's voice.

"Not for a while. I'm not totally sure. From what I understand, he really didn't trust any banks for quite a while. My grandfather said he hid the money away, mostly he bought up property and put people to work."

"Put people to work?" Hall repeated.

"Yeah, houses for the wealthy, and the not so. A couple resorts."

"Interesting. So, you don't think there's a cache of money hidden somewhere." Hall looked at the sewing box.

"I can't see how. We're talking eighty years ago. I'm sure my grandfather would have already retrieved it. He was a pretty shrewd businessman and didn't have the distrust of bankers his father had."

"You have quite the history there. I'm lucky to know my grandparent's names." He stood.

"I'm fortunate." Quinn rose with him, taking the cue to walk him to the door.

"I'll check and make sure all is done for tonight outside. Once again, if you do figure anything out let me know," Hall said as they walked through the kitchen to the backdoor.

"Will do."

"Good night, detective," Emily said from beside Quinn.

Quinn watched him go then turned to her.

"What can I do to help fix the door?" Emily asked.

Quinn knelt to inspect the damage. "I can brace it for tonight or, seeing as the door and the frame will have to be replaced, I think I'll just put some screws in it to keep it closed until I can get a new one."

While Quinn worked on that Emily went in to make dinner. After they ate, they moved into the den where Quinn started a fire in the fireplace. They settled down on the floor to explore the old trunk.

Emily ran her hand over the top. "It really is great workmanship."

"I have to agree with you. How old do you think it is?"

"I'd say easily right around a hundred years, maybe more. We'd have to research the manufacturer. But this is all hand-tooled leather and the metal corner pieces. It really is in amazing shape. If anything, the patina the metal has picked up makes it more striking."

His hand followed hers along the top, his tracing the wood. "The top looks like cherry. The slats are oak. Shall we look inside?"

"Oh, yeah." Excitement filled her face.

Once more, he did the honors of lifting the lid. Papers were piled to the top. "So how do we go about this?" Quinn asked.

"It's your call. I'd suggest we sort as we go. Pictures, letters, other papers, ledgers and books. We'll just have to see what we find."

The project drew them in. Almost an hour passed before they finished separating out the tray that held the papers. Together, they lifted out the tray to reveal another layer of treasure. Personal items filled the bottom, crocheted dollies and a baby blanket, a hand-stitched table cloth and bedspread."

“These are beautiful. They must have been made by your great-grandmother, or great-great. Wow.” She looked to him full of delight.

He felt excitement of his own. “Look at this old razor. What’s this?” He held up a glass object.

“A fairy lamp. Oh, my, it’s peachblow.” She lifted the two pieces of glass.

“That’s not peach.” He commented on the color.

“That refers to the fading color on the glass.”

“I’m thinking you really like this.”

“I do. And look at these small vases. It is cased glass and this one is ribbon glass.” She picked up the two vases and set them next to the fairy lamp.

“Pretty, but I think these interest me more.” He still studied the old straight razor. “You know, I know there are men that still prefer them, but the thought of me sticking one to my neck gives me the willies.”

“I can understand that. Look.” She pushed aside a book and lifted out a scabbard with a knife that had to have at least an eight inch blade. The initials NJL were engraved in the leather.

“Nathan James Lawson. My great-great-grandfather.” Quinn took it, turning it over in his hand. “Now this is cool.”

“Here’s a pocket knife.” She handed it to him. “And this is an older curling iron.” She pulled out a few more stitched items and postcards. Then a long dress with an incredibly tiny waist. “Wow, I wonder if this was her wedding dress. It would make sense since she saved it.”

“Looks more like an ordinary, Sunday-type dress,” he observed.

“It probably was. That was common back then to get married in your best dress. A lot of people didn’t have money or means and a lot of time to make one. They didn’t wait to do the big formal thing like we do now. It might only have been them and witnesses or they gathered family and friends, maybe even the whole town, in which case the women would bring food and they'd have a party for the send-off."

"Sounds good." He leaned forward to look in the trunk and took out some baby clothes, setting them with the dress. "Looks like we finally hit bottom." There were just a few bits and pieces of things and a couple buttons remaining.

"What's that?" Emily reached in, brushing away the stuff in a corner to reveal something gold about the size of a shirt button, but it wasn't a button.

They exchanged looks. She picked it up and handed it to Quinn who held it up so the firelight gleamed off it.

"Is that what I think it is?" Emily asked, her gaze staying with the object.

"Gold," he said the word with a slight shake of his head. "I think so."

"That's totally unexpected. Do you think your great-grandfather kept his gold in here after taking it out of the bank? That doesn't sound very secure."

"No, it doesn't. And if he took money from the bank, it wouldn't have been in gold nuggets." He looked thoughtful.

"True. Do you think he just found it and tossed it in here?"

"I'm not sure. Possibly. It doesn't seem likely." He sat quiet a minute. "There's a story I don't know much of, and if it's true," he said thoughtfully. "It was of Ethan's parents. I'd have to call my father to see if he remembers the details, but it was something about her coming west working at a railroad station. Colorado was still rough back then. She used it as a means to get here. Her father prospected gold in the Pike's Peak area. Did well, supposedly. Left it hidden and she was trying to find it." He shook his head. "I don't remember much besides my great-

great-grandfather came to her rescue, married her and together they found the gold."

"Sounds like Lawson men have always been rescuers."

"That's how we find our women." He twitched his eyebrows.

"So that's the strategy."

"It is. I guess I forgot that before now." He glanced at his watch, realizing the time. "It's too late to call my parents to get any more info tonight. In fact, we better turn in. We can start fresh tomorrow."

Mentioning that it was late induced a yawn from her. "I didn't realize." She stretched then reached for the clothing.

"Leave it. We'll continue in the morning." Taking her hand, he pulled her up with him.

"What are you going to do with that?" She nodded to the gold nugget.

"I think I'll put it in the safe so I don't lose it." He went to a painting on the wall. It swung out on hinges, revealing a safe.

"Cool, I've never seen one like that. I thought that was a movie thing."

"It comes in handy. There's a large gun safe in the storage room that I keep more stuff in."

"And guns?" she questioned.

"There are several. Most have been handed down. I'll show you sometime, if you'd like to see."

"Yes. My father was a gunsmith. I like old guns."

"Really. Do you hunt?" He turned to her as they reached the landing.

"No, but I'm a decent shot."

He arched an eyebrow. "Decent. Is there modesty or a challenge there?"

She laughed. "I don't know about challenge, but how would you feel if a woman out shot you?"

"Now, that is a challenge. You're on." He stepped closer. "And so you know, I'm okay if you out shoot me. We'll just have to make it so we both like the reward." With that he lowered his head and kissed her.

ଔ୬

"Look at this." Emily looked up from where she sat on the floor in the glow of the morning light, next to the trunk.

"What do you have?" Quinn shifted to look over her shoulder.

"A ledger. It starts in 1926. Look at this, the starting balance, which was wow, for back then. It shows his division of funds. What he put in the bank and what went into the stock market."

"This is amazing. He recorded every transaction plus," Quinn flipped several pages, "a monthly accounting of stock balances." He winced when he saw the losses in the earlier part of 1929, then let out a whistle of the amount he received in September. "Back then, that was a fortune."

"He doesn't say where he put it." Quinn started flipping more pages. "This is a list of all the land he purchased. A full accounting of who he helped. What he built. This is cool. Wait a minute, here's the purchase of a vault lock. But nothing about a vault."

They continued going through the book. He pointed to an entry. "Here's where he finally recorded moving it to bank accounts."

"But there's a discrepancy." She pointed at a number.

"I don't know. I'd have to go over it more closely to tell for sure. It might be one of the land purchases."

She sat back looking thoughtful. "You know what you said to Hall about your grandfather being a shrewd businessman, that he would have retrieved the money, if he knew about it. What if he didn't?" The idea worked its way through her mind.

"What do you mean? That his father hid money from him, too?"

"What if he didn't know? I'm not saying necessarily hid from him, but you said something earlier about a grubstake. What if his father had kept some money back – a grubstake? Like his father had. He mentioned one in the letter to Sarah." She got up to get Sarah's letter and read aloud the section again.

"Besides my grubstake, because of the dreadful incidence, I rid myself of all my investments and took all my money from the bank at a most opportune time.

I know it is not done for a man to talk about such matters with his intended or even his wife, but I want us always to be one in everything we face. I want you to know that, though my wealth is secured in gold and money, you are my greatest treasure."

"You're thinking that he held some back when he finally moved his wealth to banks."

"It makes sense. Look at this. He evidently still didn't completely trust banks. He put his money in four different ones."

"I can see what you're saying and agree it could be possible, but how would anyone know about that. And, why would they think it still exists? Especially if the family doesn't know about it."

She sighed. "Which is back where we started." She blew out. "I need to move around."

"Agreed." He stood and stretched. "Want to come help me get a new back door?"

"Sure."

ଓଃ

Emily steadied the door while Quinn shot in the first nail. A couple minutes later they stood back.

"You were right. I like it. The glass panels are a nice touch." Quinn studied it.

"I know it's different than the original."

He wrapped his arms around her. "It's okay, Emily. I wouldn't have bought it if I didn't think you were right."

"I just didn't want to be making decisions for your house."

"You have good taste. I'd be a fool not to listen."

"So what's next?" she asked.

"I need to put in the weather sealant. After that sets, I'll caulk and prep for paint."

"So nothing for me to do until we're ready to paint? I think I'm going to walk out to the memorial and weed around the bench."

Quinn stiffened. "If you'll wait a half hour, I'll go with you. I just want to finish this up."

She stretched up and kissed his cheek. "Your protectiveness is sweet, but I think I'll be all right. I'm not even leaving the property. I won't be that far away. You can join me when you finish up. It's too nice to stay in the house today." She could see the unease in him. "You'll be able to hear me if I yell."

"I'm becoming paranoid." Quinn pushed a hand up through his hair.

She laughed and stretched up to kiss his cheek again.

He snagged his arm around her waist before she could pull away. "Be careful."

Emily laughed again and broke away, going to get a pair of gloves and some garden tools before heading into the trees. It was an amazingly beautiful day. Emily didn't think she had ever been this happy before in her whole life.

She stepped into the memorial's clearing and stumbled to a stop. The shovel fell from her grasp.

Huge holes were dug all the way around the boulder. One of the rose bushes lay on the ground, the other tipped drunkenly. Tears filled her eyes. Stuffing her fist against her mouth, she managed to stifle the cry that threatened to erupt within her.

Involuntarily, she took a step forward before she stopped herself. Her gaze darting around the area. Spidery prickles ran up her back. Her breath caught.

She needed to get out of there. She needed Quinn. The thought spurred her into motion. She spun and ran, darting around trees. She stumbled, barely keeping herself from going down. Her feet never stopped moving as the fear that any moment a demon would spring from the bushes. Keeping to the path, she plowed on.

Ahead of her, the sight of the house broke through the trees and bushes. She still didn't stop. "Quinn! Quinn!" she yelled again.

He rounded the corner, muscles bunched, nostrils flaring, ready to do battle.

"Emily." He barely got out as she plowed into him. His arms went around her, pulling her tight. "What is it?" He scanned the yard beyond her.

"S…orr…y." She gasped for air, dropping her head to his chest as she fought to get herself under control. "I … frightened … myself."

"What happened? Are you all right?"

"Yes." Emily drew in a breath. "Sorry," she said one more time, blowing out then breathing deep. Her hand coming up to rest on her chest as if to control her breathing. "Someone's been at the memorial. They've been digging all round it. The rose bushes …" A tear trickled down her cheek.

He brought a hand up, brushing the moisture away. "But you're all right?"

She nodded. "Yes. I didn't see anyone." She swallowed hard. "But, I felt like someone was watching. It was probably just my imagination."

"Or maybe not. I should have gone with you." He ran his hand up and down her back.

Settling under his touch, she relaxed against him. "You can't be with me all the time, and why would you expect someone there. Who else even knows about it?"

"After all this time, I would have said only family. You're the only person I've taken out there. I don't think my parents or Payton's family have been there since last Memorial Day. I'd have to call and ask if they've shown anyone. My grandfather's gardener used to maintain it, but he'd been with my grandfather my whole life. He retired when my grandfather passed away. I didn't show the new gardeners yet, they just do the lawn and the flowers."

"You know it's seems like someone knows an awful lot about your family."

"I'm starting to realize that myself. I just don't know how. We tend to guard our privacy. There's always a concern about people trying to take advantage of us."

"I'm sorry." Emily took hold of his hand and gave it a light squeeze. "You've never seemed guarded with me."

He shifted his hand so they were palm to palm and interlocked their fingers, bringing her hand to his lips. "You slipped under my guard and into my heart the first moment I saw you."

"Oh." Her heart melted as warmth rushed through her wiping out any residual fear. "I love you." The words came without thought.

"That's a good thing because I love you." He drew her to him. "Okay." He set her away a minute later. "I better get this knob in, so we can lock up and go have a look."

❧

It only took Quinn a couple minutes to finish up. "That's good for now. I'll hook the alarm up later." He grabbed another shovel and gloves, and together they headed off through the trees.

Even though he was prepared by what Emily had said, the sight of the destruction hit him hard. He wanted to shout in anger. He pressed his lips together to keep in any retort. Still, his hands tightened into fists as his whole body went rigid. Fury and pain warred within him. This spot was special to him, just as it was to his ancestors. He couldn't say why, wouldn't even try, it just was.

Emily's light touch brushed his hand. He could feel her wanting to comfort. She understood and in that simple movement, he felt ease. His hand relaxed slightly then turned, opened, and encompassed hers. He stood for a minute more as the tension ebbed from his body, not leaving entirely but enough. With a roll of his shoulders, he released a breath and gave her hand a squeeze.

"Shall we get to work?" He looked down and forced a smile.

Moisture glistened in her eyes. She gave a slight nod, and visibly swallowed as if trying to ease her own tightened throat muscles. She was such an expressive little thing. The thought almost made him smile. It was such an antiquated thought. Something his great-grandfather would have used. It must be this spot.

"First, let's get these rose bushes back in the ground." He stepped forward. "I'll carry some water out later to ease their shock."

"They tend to be hardy. Hopefully they should be okay," she said reaching down to pick up her shovel.

He held the bushes up while she worked the dirt around their base. It only took a few minutes to have them back in the ground, and they turned their attention to filling the holes.

"Someone was searching for something." Emily commented, leaning on her shovel.

"Hidden treasure," he said with mirth though a niggling of wonder spread through him.

"But what does that have to do with the key?"

He was about to answer, when out of the corner of his eye, he caught movement. Registering it as a man, he started to turn, before he could, something struck the side of his head. Pain burst through him. His last thought was of Emily, but no matter how he tried to cling to it, everything faded into oblivion

Chapter Sixteen

A thud and a groan cut Emily off from what she was going to say. She spun around just in time to see Quinn drop to the ground. "Quinn!" she cried, diving for him. So focused on him she failed to notice the man standing off to the side of a rose bush, with a shovel in his hand, until she was already on the ground.

She screamed, draping her body over Quinn's still one to protect him.

"Who are you? What are you doing here?" The questions came out before she had time to think, then the answers came rushing in. "You dug the holes. You're the one searching. I know you. The Lawyer. Raine," she added after a second of thought.

"Yes. I would hate to think I was that forgettable to a lovely woman, though your focus has been held captivated with Lawson. It seems Lawson men have always had the power to ensnarl the most beautiful, interesting women. Isn't it funny, I would have considered you appealing?"

Emily wanted to pull back at the malice of his words, but she wasn't going to leave Quinn. "What do you want? What are you looking for?" She straightened but fear made her voice crack.

"That should be obvious. Just as Lawson said, 'buried treasure'."

Emily shook her head. Her mind not really wanting to wrap around the possibility.

"Oh, yes," he answered her unbelief. "Now, if you will hand over the key."

"I … don't have it."

"Please." He drew a gun from his pocket, moving in closer. "I would really hate to have to put a hole in Lawson."

Emily choked on her gasp. The glint of venom that flickered in his eyes screamed that the man did plan – want to put holes in him. For some reason, Raine wanted to hurt Quinn. Emily feared the only reason Quinn was still alive now was because he needed her to give him the key. "What key?" she cried out.

Anger flashed over his face. "The one you made into a necklace. The one you wear." The snap in the words made her jump.

"I don't have it on me today. I left it in the house."

"Where is it? You always wear it." There was no missing his rise agitation.

"I really did leave it in the house." Emily felt her own panic rising. "I knew I planned to be working outside and didn't want to catch it on anything."

"Then we'll have to go retrieve it, and you can tell me what you know." His ire faded. He gaze dropped to Quinn. "Tie up Lawson, just in case he wakes up."

Emily felt sick. The tone of his voice said he didn't think Quinn would ever wake again. She needed to get Raine away from him.

"I don't have anything to tie him with," she tried. Her hopes were dashed when the man reached into his pocket, pulled out a small piece of cord and tossed it at her.

"Do it and do it right."

Emily looked down, her heart breaking. Quinn was so still. Blood matted his hair.

"He's bleeding."

"He'll be bleeding more if you don't do what you're told."

Emily cringed, sliding her hands down Quinn's arms to his hands, giving them a little squeeze before bringing them together. She wrapped the cord around his wrists, not wanting to make it too tight but afraid what Raine would do if she didn't do a decent job.

Finishing, she was unable to stop herself from stroking his cheek, willing him to wake, though grateful he didn't. How hard had he been hit? The patch of blood worried her, as did his unconscious state, but his breathing seemed good. She needed to get him to the hospital.

"Move." Raine barked out making her jerk.

She started to stand.

"Stop! Get his cellphone."

Emily had to reach over Quinn, brushing her lips over his cheek as she did so. She had to shift him slightly to get it out of his back pocket.

"Okay. Toss it and yours over there." He used the tip of his gun to motion into the bushes.

Emily did so before he thought to change his mind and smash them, or turn them off, not that she'd have a chance to use them.

"All right. In front of me. Let's go and don't forget, I can put a hole in you at any time and come back to finish off Lawson."

She had no doubt that was what he planned to do, but she had to stall. Not that she knew what good it would do. "Why are you doing this?"

"I think you know. You've been searching all over the house yourself. Have you already found it and not told him? No, if you had, you'd been gone." He let out a snort. "You've been playing Lawson, haven't you?"

"I don't know what you're talking about."

"Don't you. You truly expect me to believe you just happened to buy that whole box of junk."

"That's what I do," Emily countered.

"And you just happened to end up living in his house a couple days later? It didn't take you long to work your way into his bed."

"We're not sleeping together," Emily defended.

"Right. You expect me to believe that."

Emily tried to push down the shiver the tone of his voice elicited. "Why are you doing this? What do you really hope to find?"

"The treasure, of course. It's owed me."

"Owed you?"

"Shall I tell you a story?" He didn't wait for her to answer. "All this should have been mine. Everything. Every bit of land they own."

Emily started to ask how, but he was already talking. It was like a gate of venom and hatred opened up to flow out.

"My grandfather wanted this woman. She was nothing just a simple seamstress, though young and pretty."

"Sarah," Emily whispered to herself. Her mind conjuring up the story.

"She thought if she held out, he'd marry her." Once more his tone spoke volumes, he might as well of added, "as if". "My grandfather was better than that. He could have any woman he wanted. She should've been happy with his attentions. He would have made her life comfortable. But she refused him and made a ruckus that drew Lawson's ancestor. Lawson favored her. They fought, but Lawson didn't fight fair and won."

Emily had to keep from commenting about a 'fair fight'. The man had attacked a defenseless woman. If anyone would have been fighting unfair it would've been him.

"The seamstress turned to Lawson with a sob story. The gullible fool." The sneer she couldn't see was plain by his voice. "The next week, Lawson went into the bank and made a scene wanting all his money. Demanded it in gold coin." Fury flowed from him.

"Lawson cashed out all his investments. He wiped out the bank. It didn't have time to recoup before the stock market crashed. My grandfather barely had enough to get his money."

She noticed he didn't refer to anyone else.

"But Lawson wasn't done. No, he had to buy up all the property people were getting rid of. Property that should have been my grandfather's."

"I presume the reason he also hired men, paying them wages was so your grandfather couldn't foreclose." Emily couldn't hold the comment back.

She didn't see the strike coming, fortunately, the blow that clipped the back of her head was just a glancing contact but still, it dropped her to her knees. Lights flashed in front of her eyes. Ringing echoed in her head.

"Get up," Raine's demand was followed by his foot aimed at her ribs.

Emily saw it coming and rolled to the side missing the brunt of the blow. Air whooshed from her lungs. She wondered if that was what he termed a fair fight, but kept the thought to herself, as she stumbled to her feet. The thought of making a run for it crossed her mind, but the gun pointed at her face forestalled it.

"Are you ready to continue walking?"

Emily nodded, heading to the house, keeping her pace slow to stall for more time. They'd gone about thirty feet when she spoke. "What makes you think there's a treasure? Surely he would have put the money that he didn't use to buy up property in the bank. That was nearly a century ago."

There was a soft barking sound that she supposed to be a laugh. "He didn't trust banks after that."

"Banks or bankers." Emily figured it was probably a good thing she was far enough in front of him, he couldn't reach her to smack the back of her head again.

"From what I heard, either, though he eventually moved his money to banks. Never did put money back in the stock market though. Sunk it into real estate."

"So again, what makes you think there is a hidden treasure?"

"Grandfather knew. He told me all about it and he was right. Old Lawson might have thought he was so smart, but he forgot to tell his family his hiding spot. I happened onto to it somewhat by accident. I'd hired on to the law firm that handled old man Lawson's business. Figured I'd be able to get some pay back for what was done to my family." The sneer was back. "But, ol' honest Harry, Lawson's friend always handled everything himself. I never was able to get near his dealings, after my one attempt was discovered. Though Harry never knew how the figures got messed up, he kept Lawson's files in a private safe. The paranoid old fool." Once more venom seemed to taint the air.

It hit Emily, this man spent his whole life on revenge for something that had been done, decades before he was born. She couldn't fathom it.

"But even Harrison Goodman had to retire sometime, and it just so happened that it coincided with the death of Lawson's grandfather. I volunteered to step in and handle the paper work. It was all straight forward, nothing much I could mess up. Lawson's lawyers handled most of it." The sneer was back again.

"But low and behold." His voice shifted to glee. "Grandfather was right. I found a letter, tucked in the original property description. Probably put there by mistake. A simple yellowed envelope with a letter. Explaining, just for security, he kept a 'grubstake' back, hidden away. The key to open it was in his wife sewing box. The seamstress had been dead for forty years, but he still loved her. So he hid the key to his treasure in what reminded him of her. That's why after I followed you out to the rock the other day, I thought it might be buried there and I wouldn't have to worry about the key and the map. But it wasn't."

Emily's mind rushed over everything he said. "But the sewing box –"

"That was fate." He cut her off. "I was meant to have it. To get what was owed my grandfather," he said self-righteously. "I was at the mansion. Got Lawson to give me a tour. He and his nieces were going through stuff. The girls were yammering on and on about their junk sale and collecting things for it. They had a pile set off to the side. That littlest one opened the box. I realized what it was immediately." Glee was back.

"I wanted to snatch it up right then and find the key and map, but couldn't with Lawson there. When no one was looking, I shifted it into the sale pile. There was a pile of junk jewelry in another box so I grabbed it and dumped it on top.

They stepped into the yard. Sun glistened off the house, giving it a bright cheery appeal Emily couldn't quite grasp at the moment. "What about the man who tried to steal it?"

"Did some legal work for him. He owed me. Worthless investment."

"You killed him."

"No big loss. I couldn't have him talking. I knew he wouldn't keep his mouth shut and it was only a matter of time until he was caught."

He had killed Sammy, and he was going to kill her as soon as he got the key and the map, but there wasn't a map. There was no way he'd believe that. His mind was twisted. *Think, think, think!*

The problem was she couldn't see a way out. *At least Quinn was safe.* She hoped. *Or would Raine go back and kill him when he got what he was after, or in fury that he couldn't get what he wanted? Of course, he would.*

She had to get away and call the police. She had to get to Quinn!

Chapter Seventeen

The musical notes repeated, echoing in the ringing of Quinn's mind. He shifted and groaned as the dull pain in his head flashed to agony. He started to raise his right hand and found it trapped to his left. He brought them both up together as he tried to breathe through the pain. After a minute, it settled to a dull ache.

The music started up again. This time his mind registered – his phone. It brought him more alert, and he became conscious that he was on the ground – dirt under his cheek, sun on his body and the sound of birds overhead. He forced his eyes to stay open and tried to push up only to find his hands bound? It didn't make sense. It took two attempts with a lot of groaning to make it to a sitting position. He lowered his head to his knees, breathing in and out in structured breaths to get the nausea to pass.

Raising his head, his gaze fell on the stone in front of him. *My Greatest Treasure. Emily.* "Emily!" Just calling her name made the pain in his head spike. He looked around him then at his bound wrists. Where was Emily? Who hit him and who tied him up?

"Emily." He used the boulder to make it to his feet. The world swam around him, but after a minute he was able to straighten. *He had to get his hands free and find Emily.* Using his teeth, he worked on the knot which came loose easier than he thought it would. Whoever had tied it had wanted him to be able to get free. Emily. Still his fingers tingled a little with the return of full blood flow. The rope had been tight even if the knot hadn't.

He reached for his phone finding it gone. He'd heard it. Quinn turned in a circle, not seeing it, and unfortunately now, it was silent. His mind started to catch up. Emily wouldn't have left him if he was hurt – not if she had a choice. He knew that for certain. She would have called for help. But if his phone was taken, that meant hers likely had been too. And if she wasn't here – she'd been taken.

A quick circlet through the tall grass yielded no sign of the phone. He prayed for it to ring again but it remained silent. Not wanting to waste any more time, he headed for the house in more of a stagger than a run, but he had to get help.

*

"Open it." Raine jammed the gun up under Emily's chin, making her gasp. Reaching the house and finding it locked snapped what control he still had. Rage poured from him.

Emily quashed the thought of denying the key even before it fully came to her mind. The man wasn't stable enough to challenge. Her best hope was to play along, until she had a chance to get away.

Sliding the key Quinn had given her into the lock, it hardly clicked before Raine reached around her, opened the door and shoved her in. "Put in the code." He raised the gun as if to hit her with it.

Emily pulled back but bumped against the wall. "It's not on the system, yet."

"If it goes off, you're dead." He jabbed her with the gun barrel.

She flinched, but the thought gave her an idea. This door wasn't on the alarm system but the other doors and windows were, and it was set. If she could open one of them, an alarm would go off. The problem would be getting enough time to do it without getting shot. Tears threatened.

She really was hoping on a life with Quinn. Was he all right? She had to get help.

"Where's the key?"

Raine's demand jerked her attention back. "Upstairs."

He grabbed her arm, propelling her down the hall to the stairs with the gun wedged against her side. His hold pulled her off balance and she tripped on a step as they started up. He hauled her up and kept going without pause.

They were nearing the top when she took her chance. Stumbling as if she caught her foot again, she pulled down. As he shifted to drag her up again, Emily swung back with her arm, knocking the gun away before continuing with her shoulder into his side. She ran.

The sound of the gun going off echoed through the house. Fire seared across Emily's side. She sucked in a breath but kept going, ignoring the thumping on the stairs and the yell from Raine.

Emily didn't look back. Running for the master suite, she smacked her hand on the elevator button as she passed by, hoping to draw him off. Making it to the bedroom, she closed and locked the door before going to the French doors, opening them wide before dodging into the sitting room. Closing the door behind her, she realized there was no lock.

Tiptoeing across the room to the other door, she cracked it and peeked into the hall. Empty so far. She pulled back and steeled herself to look down at her side. She wasn't surprise to see blood on her shirt. Clamping her lips tight to keep from making a sound, she eased the material away and up. Right below her ribs on her side, blood seeped from a two inch score of ripped skin. She reassured herself it wasn't bad. She'd gotten worse falling off her bike once as a kid. But it burned like crazy.

Footsteps on the stairs drew her attention back. Emily held her breath, listening as Raine limped along. "Open up!" he yelled at the master bedroom. His fist hammered against the wood adding impact to his demand.

Emily would've laughed at the absurdity that he actually thought she might comply with the demand, if it wasn't so serious. At least she didn't see the gun in his hand, but it didn't mean he didn't have it. His shoulder slammed into the door just as the house alarm split the air.

She prayed that he would flee. Instead, he smashed his shoulder into the door again, bursting it open. The moment he went inside, she ducked through the door and sprinted down the hall into her room. She snatched the key off the dresser on her way to the connecting bathroom and out the other side.

For a moment she thought about hiding in there, but the only two places would be under the bed or in the closet, and since Raine hadn't left yet, she was afraid he'd keep searching. He seemed to have slipped into manic insanity. Wanting the key and treasure was the only thing on his mind, and there would be no convincing him there wasn't one.

The sound of stuff being shoved off her dresser startled her. She hadn't heard him in the hall over the blaring of the alarm. Bolting for the door, she raced down the hall to the end bedroom.

Emily went right to the window, opening it up. Putting her head out, she considered the distance to the roof of the breezeway. It wasn't as far of a drop as she feared. She could do it easily. Swinging her leg over, pain ripped through her side as she lay on the sash. A groan escaped before she could catch it. She didn't let it slow her as she wiggled back, letting her body hang over, stretching down feeling with her toes. She lowered a bit more. Her foot brushed the shingles.

A door down the hall banged. Emily released her hold and dropped, crouching until she had herself steadied. With a hand pressed to her side and staying low, she hurried across the roof to the garage.

She was half way across when a noise had her glancing back. Raine was climbing out the window after her. He held no gun in his hand, but the glint in his eye was no less deadly.

⁂

Quinn made it to a jog as the world around him steadied. He struggled for more speed. The need to get to Emily drove him on. He couldn't lose her, he'd just found her. He wanted the future his heart promised.

Quinn lengthened his stride. He didn't know someone could mean so much to him in such a short time. But it wasn't fast for his heart. It was as if he'd known her forever. That she was the missing piece of his life.

The blare of the house alarm cut through the trees. *Emily.* Pulling on his will, he forced himself to a run. He reached the yard and started across it when he saw the figure he yearned for climb out the window onto the roof of the breezeway.. Fear of distracting her kept him from yelling out her name, then terror took over when Oliver Raine followed her out.

His still foggy mind tried to shove it all into place as he headed for the garage. It didn't make sense, but he'd worry about that later.

"Raine!" he yelled out catching the man off guard.

Raine spun and slipped, sliding almost to the edge before going to his knees to catch himself.

"Quinn." Emily turned, relief so evident on her face he could see it at the distance.

"Get to the window," Quinn yelled as he ran for the stairs, taking them two at a time.

Emily was lifting out the screen when he reached the window. In a single motion, Quinn unlocked and opened it. Wrapping his arms around her, he pulled her through, but he didn't have time for relief.

Raine crashed into them, taking them all to the floor. He locked onto Emily, trying to pull her to him and get an arm around her throat. Crying out, she rammed her elbow back, catching him in the stomach as she rolled away.

Quinn untangled himself enough to dive for the man, knocking him back. Before he could pull away, Raine was on him, going for his throat like a wild animal. Quinn's head hit the hardwood floor sending another wave of fog over his body. It was only his thought of Emily and his need to protect her that kept him from slipping back into the waiting darkness.

Quinn struck out, not even trying to aim, just to get Raine to back off. His hand connected solidly, but the pressure of the hands closing around his throat returned immediately. Light exploded like fireworks in front of his eyes, everything started to haze over.

Emily sprang on Raine, trying to wrap her arms around the insane man and pull him off. She was able to get one arm free, but Raine swung back hitting her in the side.

Emily cried out, going down again, but it gave Quinn the time he needed to catch a couple breaths and clear his mind enough to pull himself up. He drew back his fist then drove it in Raine's face putting everything he had into it.

Raine landed several feet away on his back and stayed down. Quinn slumped to the ground, conscious of Emily only a foot away. He wanted to pull her to him, but couldn't muster the movement needed to do so.

Emily managed it for him, rolling into his side. "Quinn," her whisper washed over him bringing relief. Her fingers stroked his face. His mind clung to the gentle touches, not willing to give up the feel of the caresses to slip into oblivion.

"No!" The angry shout from Raine ripped his eyes open. He tried to rise to put himself between Raine and Emily, but it wasn't necessary.

Two men stood over the lawyer, pulling his hands behind him. Quinn blinked trying to clear his mind. "What are?" It took a second to assimilate the fact that Detective Hall and another man were handcuffing Raine.

"Quinn," Emily gasped his name running her fingers over his cheeks once more. "You're okay." Her relief was palpable. "I was afraid. I thought he might've killed you. Don't you ever scare me like that again."

That brought him back. "Scare you. You scared me. When I saw you out on the roof with a man chasing you. What happened? Why was Raine trying to kill you?" He tried to sit up.

"No! Stay still." She pushed at him then dropped her head on his chest.

"You should both stay down." Detective Hall stepped over to them while the other officer held a still struggling Oliver Raine. "EMTs are on the way. And, I'd like the answer to that question also."

Emily shifted to look up but kept her arm wrapped around Quinn. "I think I can answer that, but it's crazy. He killed that man, Sammy. If you need something to hold him."

"How do you know that?" Hall asked.

"He told me," Emily said simply.

"I have a feeling this will be a very interesting story," Hall said.

Before Emily could begin, two paramedics entered directed by Officer Carlson. Beside the massive headache, Quinn was feeling much better with Emily in his arms, that was until the EMT drew her away and he saw the blood on her shirt.

"He shot you!" His exclamation made his own ears ring as he tried to break away from the man examining him to reach for her.

Hall helped grab him to keep him from lifting the hem of Emily's shirt to see for himself. Quinn started to object, but sanity caught up to him. Still, he kept his attention on her, verifying that it wasn't serious like she said. Not that he liked the thought of anything hurting her.

It was lucky for Raine, Carlson and his partner had taken him out after his rights were read. Quinn wanted to beat the daylights out of the man, not just leave him with a split lip and several loose teeth. And he, like the police, was still waiting to hear what this was all about.

Both he and Emily objected about needing to go to the hospital, but were over-ruled. Hall agreed to drive them since they refused the ambulance, and he wanted to hear the story.

Quinn wasn't happy he had to be helped down the stairs, but with Emily cuddled into his side in the back of Hall's car, he sat quietly and listened while Emily describe everything that happened. She continued her story in the waiting room still snuggled against him, barely finishing before they were taken back to see the doctor.

Quinn protested again when they were led into separate exam rooms, though they were right next to each other with just a curtain separating them. It took a lot of pleading to get the nurse to open the curtain enough that they could see each other. Quinn figured it was only to get him to calm down that they won out.

He wasn't surprised, but wasn't thrilled when he was told they wanted to admit him for observation. He knew he had a concussion, he just didn't want Emily on her own, even though the police now had Raine, who evidently was behind it all. Quinn wanted to shake his head at the craziness, but if he did, the dizziness and nausea he was experiencing would flare up. So he lay calmly in the room he'd been taken to, after the doctor cleared it for Emily to stay with him.

"You should be resting." Emily got up and circled the room.

"And you ought to settle down. The room just stopped spinning." He lifted his hand.

"Sorry." She took the offered hand and let him draw her to him. She sat on the edge of the bed. "I still have a lot of nervous energy. I really thought he was going to go back and kill you."

Quinn interlocked their fingers and brought her hand to his chest. She followed the motion, stretching down beside him.

"And all I could think of, was what happened to you." He turned his head to press his lips to her temple. "I still can't believe this was all about a ninety-year revenge and a non-existent treasure."

"It's all in Detective Hall's hands now." Emily rested her head on his chest, letting out a sigh. "You know, you really are a born rescuer."

"I told you, that's how we Lawson men find our women."

When she turned her head, the next kiss ended up on her lips.

ꕥ

Emily was zipping up her suitcase when there was a light tap on the door. "It's okay Quinn, you can come in."

He opened the door, but instead of stepping into the room he just leaned on the jam to watch her.

"I still have a headache," he said after a minute, sounding like a forlorn little boy.

Emily looked to see if he wasn't actually working his toe in circles in the carpet. "You used that argument for the last two days to get me to stay here since we left the hospital. It's time I go home."

"It was true, and I really appreciate it. If you wouldn't have stayed my mother would've been on the next plane and would have been babying me for a week."

Emily suppressed a shiver at the memory of how he'd been the first day home. Though he'd insisted he was fine, she didn't fail to notice the care in his movements and lack of appetite. She'd had aches of her own so they had taken it easy, sitting around together, watching movies, playing games. They even put together a puzzle. Some people would have called it boring, but it had been nice.

Still, she was pleased when he woke that morning starving and his normal active nature returned. "So you want me babying you?"

"You're more fun to have kiss it better." His voice said he was totally non-repentant.

"Oh." She wasn't going to complain either.

He sighed. "I'm going to miss you." He really did sound like a little boy.

It brought a smile to her. "I live like six blocks away and you have my number."

"Do you want to have dinner with me tonight?"

She laughed, but what she really wanted to say was 'yes'. "I think you'd be sick of me. I originally was only going to be staying the night, and I've been here over a week."

"Believe me, I'm not complaining."

"You were almost killed."

"No," he countered "You were almost killed. I just suffered a concussion."

She crossed to stand in front of him. If she was being honest, she really did want to stay. Especially when his hands rested on her shoulders and he started to draw her to him. Before she could figure out what to say or their lips made contact, the doorbell chimed through the house.

"Darn, and I was just going to get into some serious persuasion." He gave her a quick, light kiss before heading to the stairs.

Quinn was showing Detective Hall in as she came down carrying her suitcase.

"Headed home?" The detective nodded to the bag.

"Yes, now no one is trying to kill me," she answered.

"I think you should be good, though I'm glad I caught you still here. I think you'll want to hear this and it will save me the time of doing it twice. I guess I should have called before I came."

"What do you have?" Quinn asked, his curiosity peeked.

"A lot. Raine kept meticulous notes."

They all settled down. "What I can tell you was the gun he shot you with is, in fact, the one used to kill Sammy Wallace." He looked at her. "So with your testimony, there shouldn't be any trouble making it stick. Plus as you know we have the attempted murder, kidnapping and assault on you, witnessed by two officers. He shouldn't be going anywhere."

Emily blew out a breath.

Quinn's fingers closed over hers.

"We'd already firmed up his connection to Wallace. That was why we were headed here that day, because we discovered a tie in with you and wanted to talk to you about it. With everything that happened, we just didn't get to."

"He was the lawyer that took over the handling of my grandfather's will for the firm. I didn't know anything about the other. I'm sure my grandfather didn't either. He only dealt with his friend that I know of," Quinn said.

"That was confirmed at the law firm. Raine volunteered to take it over when the time came and no one saw any reason for him not to. He was well respected. No one guessed what was lying beneath the exterior he presented. What we've dug up is quite the tale. It seems as if his grandfather didn't marry until late in life. He was in his fifties when Raine's mother was born. I guess he was strict. Not happy his only heir was a girl. She ran away from home at seventeen and joined the hippie movement. There's no record of Raine's father or if she even knew who it was. His birth name was Ocean Rain. He added the 'e' to Rain and took his grandfather's name."

Hall shook his head. "She died of a drug overdose when he was three. The grandfather raised him after that; spoiled him, and evidently also passed on his hatred for your family. The man was wealthy enough but envied your family. We got that from an old housekeeper. The woman's ninety but can clearly remember his ranting to his grandson, calling for vengeance in his last years. The grandfather died when Raine was nineteen, just after he started college."

"Vengeance. It's sad," Emily said.

"And greed for a treasure that doesn't exist," Quinn added.

"Yeah. Destroys people all the time. But, what really brought me here today is this." He held out an envelope. "We found it in his wall-safe when searching his house. It was okayed to return it to you after we photocopied it. We figure it was taken out of your grandfather's papers. I'll go and let you read it, but I'll be in touch."

They stood along with the detective, seeing him to the door, before returning to the couch.

Quinn opened the envelope, pulling out two yellowed pieces of paper in sheet protectors. Emily leaned over his shoulder as he started to read.

To my sons,

From the moment my fair Sarah came into my life I have been blessed. Taking my money out of the exchange and bank solidified my fortune and set our way into the future when all around me was losing theirs. But I keep the lesson from my father and grandfather, a man I didn't know, but who set in action events that led my parents together and gave them a solid foundation to build on. Though, my father stressed they would have made it without it, and of that I don't doubt. My father was a fine, hardworking man and my mother matched him in faith and will. My parents loved each other.

Unfortunately, my grandfather, my mother's father, took too long to learn that lesson. He lived with a belief that wealth meant everything. It may have been the scars of war that affected him so. Whatever it was, he left his wife and young son and daughter to follow his dream of gold. He squandered most of their money to buy up claims, but against all odds, he actually did find gold. Sadly, it took nearly ten years of his life. Fearing to travel with his riches, he hid it away and finally returned to find his family, planning to bring them to Colorado.

He arrived home to find what he truly lost was worth more than all the gold he'd found. His wife and son were dead. His daughter, my mother, was being raised pretty much as a servant to strangers who had taken his farm when his wife couldn't keep it going.

He'd barely freed my mother and started to make amends when greedy men fell upon him. They murdered him in an effort to learn the secret of his hidden gold. This knowledge nearly cost my mother her life also. Only by her courage, and the honor and protection of my father, did she survive to enjoy the love they found together.

They made a good life here for twenty and five years before heading on to California to be closer to my two sisters. My father gave me the land here and a portion of their wealth, gold remaining from my grandfather, as a grubstake. He also gave me a far greater gift. The advice that all the gold in Colorado was not worth a fraction of the treasure of his heart – my mother.

So I leave you my grubstake and the small remaining portion of the gold that led us to this place. I've held this back in case once again the economy fails our country. I also give you counsel, that you will not fail in life if you find and marry your own greatest treasure as I and my father before me did.

The key is where it has always been kept, in my fair Sarah's sewing box. The grubstake is where I received My

Greatest Treasure's heart. Now I can only sit and remember each moment I spent with her and dream of holding her in my arms again.

Live well. Be happy and know you have a rich heritage of love behind you.

Your father, Ethan Lawson Aug 24th 1956

Quinn swallowed, lowering the papers. "This would have been written to my grandfather and his brother Owen who died in the Korean War."

Emily wiped moisture from her cheek. "What an amazing history. Your great-grandfather was a remarkable man."

"Yes." He smiled at her, then went serious. "I guess we can see where Raine thought there was a treasure. He just didn't take into account that was more than sixty years ago. Three generations."

"He also missed that this letter, and the stories in it, tells what the true treasure is. It substantiates your family legends. What an amazing heritage."

He wrapped his arm around her shoulder. They sat like that for a while.

Finally he sighed, pressed a kiss to her forehead and stood. "Let's go send a copy of this to my parents and Payton."

As they crossed the entryway, his gaze landed on her suitcase. "You really are going to make me let you go home."

"I really have to."

"And I don't have to like it." He grinned. "Dinner?"

"Yes. I'd volunteer to cook, but I don't have any food at my place."

"Tomorrow there. I'll take you out tonight."

Chapter Eighteen

"This is it, the last box." Quinn came in and lowered the box marked dishes on to the counter.

"Now, I just have to unpack everything." Emily grinned back.

"How about we take a break and go for a walk?" He could see the spark the idea lit in her mind and pressed on. "Come on. My parents will be here in an hour. Tomorrow's the Fourth. You're not going to get much done then. You can just stay in the house tonight and have kitchen privileges."

"I take it I'm making breakfast?"

"If you insist." He caught her hand leading her down the stairs.

She made no comment when they took the path toward the rock. They'd taken up walking that way at least once a week.

"I heard from Detective Hall earlier today. He said Raine is going for an insanity plea."

"He might get it," she said.

"Yeah, well even if he does, he won't get out in his life time."

"Which is a relief. I don't want him to be able to get anywhere near you."

"Likewise," Quinn agreed, tightening his arm around her waist. He liked how easily her stride matched his.

"You know, in a way though, I have to be grateful to him."

"Oh?" His eyebrow raised as he looked at her.

"Without him, I might not have met you," she pointed out.

"No," he said vehemently. "I noticed you the moment you walked across the yard. I would have figured out some way to meet you. The sewing box just made it easier." He smiled as he led her to Sarah's boulder, motioning her down on it. He dropped to a knee before her.

Emily's eyes widened.

Quinn reached into his pocket. "You know we read in Ethan's letter that he thought that it was fate that he was there to rescue Sarah, that she was the love of his life? I believe I was to meet you, and that you are the love of my life. Emily, will you marry me and be mine forever?" He opened the box revealing a large diamond haloed with a ring of smaller ones in an elegant vintage type setting of white and yellow gold that spoke of old and new.

"Oh." Her hands raised to cover her mouth.

"Emily, I know we haven't known each other long, but I want to spend the rest of my life with you."

"I love you." She blinked couple times, holding in the moisture that sparkled in her eyes.

"Is that a yes?"

"Oh, yes. Forever." She held her hand out to him.

The moment he slid the ring on her finger, she slipped off the rock, into his arms. Emily's arms wrapped around his neck as their lips met.

Quinn was lying flat on his back, with her laying on him, breathing hard when the kiss finally ended. He brushed her hair back, then cupped her face as he smiled up at her. "Have I told you how much I like how you kiss?"

"Funny, I was just thinking the same about you." She kissed him again.

He sighed, nuzzling her cheek. “We’re just good together.”

“Yes.” Her heart seemed to be carried on that one word.

“I like the sound of that.”

She laughed, kissing him again.

“You know how Nathan and Sarah didn’t wait long to get married. Would you mind a short engagement? Again, I know we haven’t known each other long, but I really do miss having you in the house. I know you’ll be above the garage but that’s almost worse, knowing you’re so close but not with me. Boy, that didn’t sound very romantic, did it.”

She framed his face with her hands. “It sounded truthful. And I understand the feeling. I think we can talk about a short engagement, or we could just elope.”

“I’m for that, but my mother might not forgive us. Speaking of which, we better get back. My parents will be here anytime and I want to introduce them to their new daughter-in-law to be. Though, I think they’ve already figured it out.”

“I hope they are okay with it.” She planted her hands to his chest to push up.

“Oh yeah, my Mom let me know before she left last month that she thought you were ‘good for me’. Her words, honest.”

“I’m glad. I like your parents.”

“Good.”

Emily started to roll off but he locked his arm down, holding her for one more kiss before letting her go. When he released her, she shifted off to kneel beside him, smiling down.

“You know.” He looked up at the clear blue sky. “The last time I lay on the ground here, I was afraid I’d lost you. This feeling is much better.” He started to roll to the side to get up and froze.

"Quinn?"

He lowered onto his stomach and army crawled to the bench. Reaching out he traced the carving near the bottom of the leg. He brushed his finger over the hole in the granite then moved to the other leg and did the same thing. Pulling out his pocket knife, he cleared dirt away that had built up as Emily settled back down beside him.

They exchanged looks.

"Can I see the key?" His chest felt tight.

Emily brought it over her head. She'd forgotten she'd put it on that morning, though it had become one of her favorite pieces of jewelry. She handed it over and watched as Quinn carefully moved the crystals and charms out of the way before fitting the key into the hole.

They exchanged glances one more time before he applied pressure. The key turned with a slight grinding then there was a click. Quinn removed it and turned to the other side. There was more resistance this time, but finally it gave.

"Okay." He breathed out. Together they stood, each taking a side of the bench and lifting. It was almost a shock when the base actually came up like the lid of a box. As one, they set it aside and looked down.

What looked like a solid piece of stone was actually hollowed out. The opening was only about a foot and a half long by eight or nine inches wide and four inches deep. It was mostly empty except for three pouches. The smallest one was tanned leather about the size of Emily's palm with a leather drawstring cinched tight. The other two were larger bags. Each about the size of a small cantaloupe and a tie wrapped around the top holding it closed.

Getting on his knees once more, Quinn lifted the smaller out first. Carefully, he worked open the leather ties. He looked inside then up at Emily.

"What is it?" she asked in a hushed voice.

"Treasure." He grinned, and tipped several pebble sized nuggets of gold into his hand.

"Wow. That's got to be from like your great-great-grandfather. The original gold."

"I think you're right." He poured them back in the pouch, closed it up and handed it to her before reaching for one of the bigger bags. "It's heavy."

"You think it's full of gold, too?" Emily asked as he worked on the tie.

"It feels like coins."

"Silver dollars?" Her voice rang with excitement.

He got the knot free and looked inside. "Dollars, but not silver." He started to reach in but she caught his hand, holding it back. "No, don't touch them."

"What?"

"I think we should be wearing gloves before we handle them."

"Why?"

"The coins I see on top are Saint-Gaudens double eagles, twenty-dollar gold pieces. It looks like they all are, if the ones in rolls are the same."

"How do you know that?" Her obvious awe beginning to affect him.

"I used to go to coins shows with my father when I was a kid. They were one of my favorite coins. They're beautiful."

"And I take it they're worth a lot?"

"Oh yeah. Raine's treasure may be worth a lot more than even he thought. There's got to be well over a hundred coins there, and each one is easily worth well over a thousand dollars, maybe two, just for the price of gold. Depending on the year, the mint and the grade, you could have single coins worth twenty-five thousand or more. You'd have to have someone qualified to grade them take a look. What's in the other bag?"

Quinn set the bag back in the box and picked up the other, opening it. "It's not as heavy. It looks like a combination. This one has a lot of rolls beside loose coins. Ten dollar, five, two and a half?" He looked up questioning.

She nodded. "They're called quarter Eagles, I think. Their designs look like both Liberties and Indians." She swallowed. "Raine said something about Ethen demanding all the money in coin. Cleared out the bank. There's probably three, four hundred coins. Quinn, I'd guess you're looking … at least … around a half million dollars. And that may be real low."

He looked down and blew out a breath. "Let's get this back to the house." He lifted the pouch with the nuggets and put it in his pocket. They positioned the bench back in place and reengaging the locks, then he handed her the lighter bag while he took the heavier.

Emily nestled hers in the crook of her arm. "I know this sounds funny, but try not to jostle them around so they don't rub on each other."

"Okay." He accepted easily, shifting the bag so it rested cradled like the one in her arm. "So tell me about this grading you mentioned?" he asked as they walked.

"It's based on how much wear there has been on the coin. There are poor, which is basically you can tell it's the coin. Good and very good are your lower. Then you get into the mid-range which is fine and very fine," she explained. "And the real nice are AU, which is about uncirculated, and Unc, uncirculated. The coin we saw on top looked like it might be an AU, but I don't know. They also have a number system, but I don't remember it."

"Well, we'll take a look and see what we have when we get home, then after the holiday I'll get someone in that knows. I have to admit I think they're kind of cool."

"Same here. I just can't believe it."

"You can't This is my family. I'm sure my father doesn't know and I don't think my grandfather ever put it together. If he did, he probably thought his father had already moved it or just forgot about it."

"And it became part of legend." She smiled up. "Your family really has a remarkable one."

"There you two are," Quinn's father, Nathan called out as they broke through the trees. "Wondered where you got off to. Should have guessed." The man who looked like an older version of Quinn came toward them across the patio. "Looks like you got her all moved."

"Except for her couch and a couple things I was hoping you would help me with in the morning," Quinn answered in the way of greeting.

"I think we can do that," his father returned.

"What do you have there?" Catherine, his mother, asked as they neared, motioning to the bags.

Quinn grinned. "Treasure," he said simply, bringing a laugh from Emily.

"How was your trip?" Quinn asked, reaching the couple. He pressed a kiss on his mother's cheek.

Emily received a similar greeting with a one arm hug.

"Good. Now, what is this treasure?" his father asked.

"Come on in the house and we'll show you." He led the way through the house to the den. "You know the legend and the letters. It looks like there is a lot more truth then we knew."

He carefully set the bag on the desk along with Emily's, and then pulled the pouch from his pocket. Once more, tipping a few nuggets into his hand.

"Is that gold nuggets, like the one in the trunk?" his mother asked.

"It is. We're guessing from the original stash." Quinn held them out for her to see.

"Don't tell me that's all …" His father broke off, his eyes going wide.

"Kind of." Quinn set the pouch and nuggets on the desk then took his time opening the bag, feeling the drama.

When he opened it enough so they could see in, both his parents gasped.

"You can't be serious." His father reached out.

"Uh-huh." Quinn halted him. "Emily says we shouldn't handle them until we know how to."

Nathan looked to her.

"Dirt and oils from our fingers are not good for them. We should at least wash up first. Then we need to handle them only on their edges, never the front. That's about all I know." Emily smiled under their wide-eyed look

"Then let's find out what's the proper way." Quinn's mother went to the computer. A minute later, she gave directions and they all cleaned their hands.

"You know, instead of just putting them on the desk, why don't we put them on trays that I can put in the safe, so we're not taking them in and out of the bag?" Quinn suggested.

"Good idea, and it suggested putting them on a soft cloth," his father added.

"I know where there should be some if you haven't moved them," Catherine said, going to get them, while Quinn gathered some serving trays.

With everything in place, they settled down to go through the bag.

"You first." Quinn looked at Emily. "You're the only one with any experience, and you found the key."

Emily bit her lip and started to open the bag.

"Wait a minute." Catherine halted Emily just as she started to reach inside. "What's this?" Catherine caught Emily's left hand lifting it up to examine the ring on her finger. "You didn't tell us."

Emily looked at Quinn, her eyes filling with mirth. "It just happened. I think we forgot."

They started to laugh. The coins were put on hold for hugs and congratulations.

“So when are you thinking?” Catherine asked, directing the question to Emily as they settled around the desk once more.

It was Quinn that answered. “As soon as we possibly can, and still have it nice.”

“What do you mean as soon?” his mother asked.

“A month,” Quinn asked with a hopeful look.

“Quinn.” Emily and his mother echoed his name.

The women exchanged looks and grinned.

“We are really going to have to get working on this,” his mother said.

Nathan laughed, slapping his son on the back. “I know exactly how you feel. But one thing your mother excels at, is how to plan a party in no time. We can make it in a month.”

“Month and a half,” his mother said firmly as Emily lifted out the first coin.

It took three hours to lay out and record all the coins’ dates and mints. By the time the tally was finished, they had two hundred twenty-dollar gold pieces; a hundred and fifty ten-dollar; two hundred five-dollar; and two hundred two-and-a-half-dollar. All were minted from in the 1860’s to 1929 and were from every the mints Emily could remember existing.

Catherine leaned back. “You know, I’m feeling a little overwhelmed. They’re beautiful. And five thousand dollars.”

“That was a lot of money back then. It would have paid for a house and a car,” Emily exclaimed a little awed. “A loaf of bread or a gallon of gas was like ten cents.”

“He wanted to take care of his family,” Nathan said with a shrug of his shoulders.

“He was a smart man, who didn’t entirely trust banks.” Quinn winked at Emily.

"Yes, well." His mother stood. "I suggest you lock this away in the safe for the night. I'm going to head to bed."

Nathan stood, stretched, and slid his arm around his wife's waist. "I'll say good night, also. See you in the morning."

"Emily agreed to make crepes for breakfast," Quinn said as they started out of the room.

"I'll look forward to it. Goodnight," Catherine said walking out. "Congratulations on the engagement, not the coins if I need to clarify."

"Goodnight," Quinn and Emily said in unison.

Emily helped him settle the trays of coins in the safe, then started to turn the lights off. She stopped at the reading light next to the chair by the fire place and knelt down by Sarah's sewing box. Since she finished the touches of restoration the wood gleamed in the light with a glow of its own.

She ran her finger over the inlaid wood. "I figured out what the sewing kit is really worth," she said staring at it.

"Oh, really. What?" Quinn came to stand over her, placing his hands on her shoulders.

"I'm thinking – a life time together." She turned her head to look up at him.

Silently, Quinn helped her up so she was standing in front of him. "I can agree with that. Raine had it all wrong. The gold wasn't the treasure. You are. You are my treasure." He eased her into his arms and into a kiss.

About the Author

I grew up in a small town in Wyoming loving the outdoors, sports, art, and reading Hardy Boys books. After reading them all at least a half dozen times, I started writing my own stories.

For thirty-three years I was married to a wonderful, honorable man. I'm mother of five children and a grandmother. I love traveling. Through my husband's work and vacations, I have visited much of the United States, all over Europe, Canada, Mexico, China, Thailand, Cambodia and Australia, giving me many intriguing locations and experiences for my stories.

I am a storyteller. I write the classic hero story because I think there's a need for more heroes, love, and adventure in our lives. I'm not out to change the world with my writing; I'm just hoping to make your day a little better.

Hope you enjoy.
Alysia S. Knight

Please feel free to visit me through my website:
WWW.ALYSIASKNIGHT.COM

www.ingramcontent.com/pod-product-compliance
Lightning Source LLC
LaVergne TN
LVHW091145080826
845145LV00008B/2258